Searching for Joy

Searching
for Joy

Tim Barretto

Beech River Books
Center Ossipee, New Hampshire

B℟B

Beech River Books
P.O. Box 62, Center Ossipee, N.H. 03814
603-539-3537
www.beechriverbooks.com

LIBRARY OF CONGRESS CATALOGING-IN-PUBLICATION DATA

Barretto, Tim.
Searching for joy / Tim Barretto. -- 1st ed.
p. cm.
Summary: "A novel about an architect facing the dangers of cancer,
which emphasizes the relationship of fathers and sons. With vivid
scenes of skiing, fly-fishing, and the complicated tensions of family,
Barretto (a UNH writing professor), shows how enjoying life and
having a passion for living is one of the finer gifts one generation can
pass on to another"--Provided by publisher.
ISBN-13: 978-0-9793778-4-6 (pbk. : alk. paper)
ISBN-10: 0-9793778-4-6 (pbk. : alk. paper)
1. Architects--Fiction. 2. Cancer--Patients--Fiction. 3. Fathers and
sons--Fiction. I. Title.

PS3602.A8368S43 2007
813'.6--dc22
2007015766

Printed in the United States of America

This book is for my father, Gene, and for my sons,
Nick and Chris, who have helped me to understand
the joys of family and the enduring connections
between father and son — through hiking and
skiing in the mountains; fly fishing for trout;
watching, coaching and playing baseball (with
particular emphasis on the Red Sox in the first two
respects!); and celebrating the inevitable passage of
one generation into the next.

Contents

I went to the woods because I wished to live deliberately, to front only the essential facts of life, and see if I could not learn what it had to teach, and not, when I came to die, discover that I had not lived. I did not wish to live what was not life, living is so dear... I wanted to live deep and suck out all the marrow of life... to put to rout all that was not life...

— Henry David Thoreau

Chapter One

A Fine Day

Tom loved the smell of trout frying in a pan. Dipped in egg batter and rolled in seasoned flour and cornmeal, the freshly caught trout sizzled before him on the stove in a pool of melted butter as he recalled the day: the quiet and the darkness of early morning when he awoke to fix breakfast for his son, Ben, and himself; the cold press of his waders as he eased into the blueblack river before dawn and witnessed the sun burnish the pink of the eastern horizon into gold; the long controlled arcs of Ben's fly line before it fell softly to the surface and floated a dry fly, usually a grasshopper, past cutaway banks of the river; the swirls and the rings and the abrupt splashes of trout rising to flies, and the suddenly taut line and the bent rod, his splendid bamboo rod, his heart racing in surprise each time he felt the electric life of a fish on his line—as if each time were the first; the slanting rays of the late-September northern sun and the brilliantly colored trees along the river, leaves shimmering in the breeze and the dappled yellow light; and now this—the smell and the sound of their efforts and their pleasure palpably in front of him. It had been an altogether fine day. A day to remember, Tom realized as he listened to Ben singing in the shower. A day that was about as much as he had any right to ask for.

*   *   *

And it had almost not happened. It was only through Fran's incessant cajoling in the first place that he had finally asked Ben to join him on this brief trip to Pittsburg to fish the Upper Connecticut. At twenty-six, with a beautiful wife and three year old son, and in his first September of his first year teaching high school English, Ben possessed precious little free time to go fishing. He was, he said, spending many hours every weekend reading papers and preparing ways to stay "just barely ahead" of his students. Tom had felt guilty even asking his son to join him, all the more so when he experienced another of those bouts of not feeling well and almost called Ben to cancel the trip. He was glad now that he hadn't, and that Ben knew nothing of what had almost happened.

Listening to Ben singing in the shower, he remembered how earlier in the day he had crested the bank of the river quietly and come upon Ben by chance, having no preconceived intention of spying on him as he fished; it seemed to Tom there was something improper or deceptive, almost an invasion of personal privacy, about stopping for more than a clandestine moment to watch his son wading there in the middle of the river beneath him, and yet he could not pull himself away. Ben was thigh deep in a wide, clear stretch of river where the fast-moving current rippled around him, the water dark below and fir green at the edges where it reflected the hemlocks and spruce that lined the bank. Ben's casts were sure and patient, his fly line arcing gracefully behind him with his rod never bending beyond one o'clock before a quick, forceful snap of the wrist sent the line rolling out straight and soft before him, the fly coming to rest lightly on the surface as Ben kept his unwavering gaze focused forward on a spot where, after a moment, Tom understood from the telltale rings a fish was rising, chasing insects upstream just ahead of Ben's casts. Ben moved upriver soundlessly, stripping line from his reel as he waded forward, feeling his way along with slow and patient care and disturbing the river as little as possible in his pursuit of the fish, which from the size of its head and the rings it left behind was a fine and formidable one. Tom watched for several moments longer admiring the beauty of Ben's casts and the circumspection of his movements, as though Ben moved out of a kind of reverence for the ritual harmonies of his surroundings, and if the pace of his locomotion were such that he could not quite reach the fish without creating a stir—a hurried splash of the river or a wild back cast and a snagged tree branch—then it was perhaps simply not his right to catch this particular fish at this particular time. There would be other times. The fish seemed to have disappeared even as Tom stood there wishing for his son's success, yet instead of feeling disappointment at a missed opportunity Tom found himself admiring his son's discipline, felt flush with a kind of unalloyed pride and wished there were some way to convey that to Ben without revealing that he had stood there watching his son in private for several moments. But he knew that would not happen. It must, simply, be enough for him to have been a witness at all.

"Ben, are you almost through in there?" he called, interrupting his own reveries. "The trout have just about finished cooking and everything else is ready."

Tom had sweet onions simmering on another burner, just-picked green beans coming to a boil, home-fry potatoes being kept warm in the oven, and sliced tomatoes seasoned in a bit of olive oil with salt and pepper and fresh basil spread out on a large platter. It gave him great pleasure to prepare food for his son, and except for the trout, all of it had come from his own garden, which made tonight's meal an even more satisfying offering.

Ben's singing ceased and Tom heard the water abruptly turned off, followed by the quick shake of the pipes in response, as if the free flow of water in this old cabin could not be contained without a struggle. In a moment the bathroom door opened and Ben, towel wrapped around his waist, stepped quickly away from the swirling steam into the nearby bedroom. "I'll be right out," he called. "Smells good in there."

"You left the light on," Tom said as he crossed the kitchen to turn it off.

"I'll get it when I come out."

"Why not just do it when you leave the room, like most normal people?"

Ben either did not hear or chose not to reply, and Tom shook his head with a kind of wry satisfaction. Some things would never change. Ben had been doing this all his life—leaving lights, including car headlights, on; leaving lids or caps off (Tom had once attempted to shake a bottle of salad dressing after Ben had used it, only to have the top fly off and dressing shoot straight up into his face—funny now, but at the time Tom had not been amused); closing the freezer door only part way, or allowing a half gallon of ice cream to remain out on a counter overnight; using tools from the workshop and failing to put them away (Tom had once found an expensive crosscut saw out in the woods behind the house, rusted beyond use); melting butter in a frying pan over a lit burner, and then walking away and forgetting about it—that one had resulted in a minor but memorable fire in the kitchen. Ben's intentions were never to cause harm, but the modus operandi was always the same: not following a thing through to its completion, often based on the feel-good assumption that it would get done *later*, that there would always be plenty of time to finish the task *later*.

Tom wondered how Ben would ever manage as a teacher, let alone as a father, having to deal not only with his own strong penchant for procrastination but also with the countless missed or tardy assignments and feeble excuses his students would undoubtedly present to him. Would he be tolerant of his students' lapses and failures because of his personal struggles with the twin demons of organization and timeliness? Would he change his ways and become a model of responsibility, while holding his students accountable for the same? Or would he waffle in hypocrisy, as it seemed so many did nowadays, expecting more of others than he expected of himself? Tom found this last possibility disturbing, and did not believe Ben would ever sink so low, but there was plenty of evidence in the world today of people expecting that life owed them something, as if by virtue of being alive, by the simple biological functions of blood coursing through their veins and breath pumping oxygen into their lungs they must be accommodated, their lives must be sustained, and not just sustained but enriched. It seemed now to be the way of the world: expecting more from life, and from others, than one gave back.

"That looks great," Ben said, drawing near the stove and sniffing the air with exaggerated pleasure. "And the smell...mmmm...as the kids today would say, 'It's to die for.' Now what can I do here?"

Tom looked over his shoulder at his son standing near, amused and chuckling inwardly at the ease with which a few years and a responsible job could transform one of the kids today into a commentator on "kids today." At about five foot eight Ben was nearly four inches shorter than Tom, an immutable fact now in Ben's adult life, and Tom wondered if it bothered him. For a long time, beginning even before the arrogant certainty of the teenage years, Ben would proclaim with fervor and unalloyed confidence, "I'm going to be taller than you, Dad." "Not a chance," Tom would insist, half meaning it. The "Dad" of Ben's prediction gave way at some point, after Ben had grown a bit, to the more playfully disrespectful "old man" and was usually accompanied by a poke or a jab to Tom's midsection. But the prediction hadn't come true, and Tom felt sorry that it hadn't—he wished, more than Ben would ever know, that he had been able to give his son what he wanted. The matter of height aside, what Tom saw in Ben now was a handsome young man with wavy (his mother's gift to him) dark hair, wet still from his shower, a clear, honest, intelligent face as yet unmarred by the cynicism Tom had felt for so much of his own life, and earnest, thoughtful blue eyes, eyes that would lock onto a person and search, with polite candor, for the meaning not just of the person's words but of the person. Tom was very proud of his son, though he generally found himself at a loss for ways to express it, and often worried over whether Ben had any idea how intensely he felt this. He had been demanding of Ben throughout his life—had called him to task for the smallest things, had spoken harshly to him more as a rule than as an exception—and he feared that Ben might not understand he wanted only for his son to develop the kind of toughness and resilience that would keep him safe, secure him passage through life without being too badly wounded.

"I think I've got everything under control, but how about a beer? You want a beer?"

"Sure."

"Why don't you get us a couple out of the fridge. I brought up some home brew. The good stuff—brown ale."

"Great. Thanks." Ben found a couple of glasses in a cupboard and took two bottles from the refrigerator and held them up to the light. They were clear glass tavern bottles that allowed him to admire the clarity and the rich dark brown-amber color of the ale. "Nice," he said.

Ben used the Swiss Army knife that he carried with him at all times to take off the caps before pouring each bottle into a glass, careful to preserve the ale's clarity by leaving its sediment at the bottom of the bottle. "You know, you can drink this stuff."

"What's that, the sediment?"

"Yeah. Surprisingly, it doesn't taste too bad, and it's supposed to have a lot vitamins or something in it that are actually good for you."

"I've heard that, but I've never been too interested."

As if to prove his point, Ben slugged down the remaining contents of one of the bottles. "Here you go," he said, holding out a glass to his father.

"Thanks," Tom said, turning from the stove to take the glass. He held it head high before him. "Cheers. To a fine day of fishing. I'm glad we could both be here."

"Cheers," Ben agreed, clinking his glass to his father's before they each took a drink. Ben turned the glass of ale in his hand and gave an approving nod. "This is nice. So you're still brewing these days?"

"No, no, I haven't had time. I probably haven't brewed in over a year. This is from a batch I stashed away for special occasions. It's about two years old—like me, you know? Well aged." They both laughed.

"The 'aged' part I could agree with. But I don't know about the 'well.'"

"I thought you said you liked it."

"I do." They both laughed again.

Tom did not want to tell Ben that the reason he hadn't been brewing had less to do with time than it did with energy. At nearly sixty he had found himself slowing down in ways he never would have believed possible even just a year or two before. It seemed as if he needed more sleep and got less done each day, and there were some days when he did not even feel like getting out of bed. Fran attributed these things to a kind of general depression, or delayed midlife crisis, although she urged him to see a doctor to figure out whether or not the cause was something physical. He found it curious that she would suggest this because he *had* been experiencing physical problems also, but he had not let on about them even to her.

He wasn't sure exactly how long it had been happening, because the problem had developed over the past few months, but for some time now he had been having difficulty with the simple act of urinating. There were times when the urge was so great he felt as if his bladder were about to explode, as if the bladder had expanded to the size and tautness of a basketball—and he had come to understand all too well what the expression "piss like a racehorse" *felt* like, even though the slow, intermittent stream and lack of volume that issued from him belied the feeling. But he had always prided himself on his ability to hold it in, *not* to be like Fran and most of the other women he had known in his life whom he would playfully accuse of being unable to go on a car trip without having to stop every half hour, and so he never let on to her or anyone else. Just on this ride up to Pittsburgh from Portsmouth, a four hour trip, he had felt that sudden powerful urge at least half a dozen times and been forced to swerve to the side of the road to relieve himself at the edge of the woods. Once he could not even make it to the woods and had to hide himself behind the passenger side of the car.

Fishing in waders today had not been easy—the urge hit him sometimes in the middle of the river, and it was all he could do to get himself safely back to shore where he could roll down his waders and let loose, although invariably he could not piss it all out and would wet himself a little. He tried to keep out of Ben's view so that Ben would not know how frequently he had to relieve himself—but he was tormented by the not-too-farfetched notion of pissing into his own boots, or even worse, slipping and falling in his rush to get back to shore, having his waders fill up with water, and being swept away, drowning, somewhere downriver. He tried to make light of it by imagining macabre headlines: "Fly Fisherman Pisses Himself Off"; "Fisherman Pisses It All Away in River"; "Pissed to Death!" He could even see the lead: "In a desperate but ultimately futile attempt to reach that great lavatory at the edge of the river, fly fisherman Tom Derringer couldn't quite make it. After urinating in his waders and thereby weighing himself down beyond hope, he was swept downriver to an untimely death by drowning."

It was funny, but it was no joke, really—it had changed his sex life without question. He no longer felt at ease initiating lovemaking with Fran when he was filled with the fear—the real, visceral fear—that he would start to piss at any moment. At some level that he did not want to examine too closely it seemed his libido was changing, or had changed, and whether this was the product of a generally aging physiology or the specific consequence of his urinary difficulties, he did not know. He only knew that he—Tom Derringer, dubbed "TD, the Score King" by some of his wise-ass buddies for his sexual adventures in high school and college—he, of all people, did not want to have sex anywhere near as often as he used to, and he hoped it had not become obvious enough that Fran had noticed it too.

Often, especially in recent weeks, he had also been experiencing back pains. They would come on with no warning, unpredictably, so sharp and so severe they would suddenly double him over. This he could not always hide from Fran, so she would give him a massage, which sometimes helped and sometimes seemed to make the pain worse. It was the back pain more than anything else that had almost kept him from coming up to fish with Ben, but Fran had finally convinced him that he needed to get out, that he couldn't just stay home and be miserable. She also urged him—as she had done several times before—to see a doctor about his back, but he dismissed the idea once again, attributing his problems to injuries suffered long ago as a result of the many hard manual labor jobs he had worked during summers as a teenager. It was possible, he admitted, that he might have developed some kind of arthritis due to those injuries, but there was little doctors could do about that anyway other than to prescribe anti-inflammatory medications, which he could easily provide for himself without the high cost of their meddling. Fran finally gave him the ultimatum that either he go fishing with Ben, which would do him a lot of good despite himself, or she was going to call Ben and tell him what was going on.

"Well, let's sit down and eat," Tom said. He turned off all the burners. "Have a seat."

"I can serve myself."

"Relax."

"No, seriously. You don't have to serve me."

"Relax, I said. Everything's under control here. Just sit back and enjoy."

Ben reluctantly took a seat, thinking that some things would never change. His father would always want control, and he would always resent it no matter where they were or what they were doing. He watched with a mixture of bitterness and admiration as his father took one of the trout from the frying pan and centered it on a plate, then neatly arranged the green beans, the home fries and the onions around it.

"Here you go, Ben," Tom said as he placed the plate before his son. "I think everything else you need is out—butter, salt and pepper, ketchup..."

"So I see."

"Go ahead and dig in. Don't wait for me, I'll be right with you."

Ben waited and watched as his father, consistent in his fastidiousness, prepared his own plate just as he had prepared Ben's. When he turned from the stove and was about to sit down, though, he winced and pitched forward, nearly dropping his plate to the floor. One hand shot behind him and held his back as he eased himself down into the kitchen chair and took a deep breath.

"What's the matter, old man?" Ben asked, not wanting to sound either too alarmed or too cavalier, and yet not wanting to ignore what he had just seen.

"Nothing. I'm all right."

"You almost lost your dinner."

"Just had a little twinge in my back. It's no big deal. *Eat.*"

It occurred to Ben that his father looked quite a bit older than he had just a couple of months ago when they had last seen each other, or perhaps it was that Ben was suddenly paying closer attention now than he had then. Without question there seemed to be more white in his father's thinning dark hair, and the creases in his forehead and around his brown eyes seemed deeper, but what struck Ben most forcefully was the generally haggard look to his father, as if he had lost weight. His father had always been on the thin side, a slim, handsome man of six feet who had always kept himself in excellent physical condition, had always taken pride in his ability to stay in shape while other men his age gave up the battle. But now there was a hollow look to his cheeks, his clothes appeared a little too slack, his shoulders seemed slumped as he fussed with his trout to separate it into neat halves. There were age spots beginning to show on the backs of his hands.

"What are you looking at? Eat, will you?"

"Have you lost weight, old man?"

"Of course not."

"You look like you have."

"You're wasting a good fish with all this talking." Tom glanced up and gestured toward his son's plate. "Come on. Everything will go cold."

Ben began to eat but kept his eyes on his father. "I just want a straight answer. I don't think you're being honest."

"When you get to be my age, not everything works the way it used to, okay? Lately I've been having a little back pain once in a while, probably the result of working at the quarry when I was a teenager—you know, those stories you could never stand hearing about how tough I had it compared to you? I maybe have a touch of arthritis from that that flares up every so often. That's it, end of story."

When you get to be my age. Ben never would have believed he'd hear these words from his father, especially not at age sixty. "How long has it been going on?"

Tom gently placed his knife and fork down on his plate, folded his hands, and looked squarely at his son. "Look, I didn't come up here to answer twenty questions about my back or any other part of my anatomy. So I'd appreciate it if we could stop talking about my health and get back to enjoying the meal we presumably came up here to enjoy."

Ben thought about this for a moment. "So what other part of your anatomy is bothering you?" he said, straight-faced.

"The asshole I have for a son," his father deadpanned.

Chapter Two

Sounds and Silences

"Your father hasn't called you yet?" his mother asked, after the obligatory questions about Marie and Teddy.

"No. Why?"

"He promised me he would. He said he would definitely call last night."

"Well I was here all night grading papers and the phone never rang." Ben could sense his mother's concern in the silence at the other end. "Mom, what's wrong?"

"I'm not sure," she said hesitantly. "I'm trying not to be an alarmist. Did you notice anything unusual about your father last month when you two went fishing?"

Ben thought about this for a moment. "Not really. Although at one point he did have some trouble with his back. And I told him I thought he might have lost a little weight. But otherwise no, I didn't see anything unusual. Why?"

There was a long pause at the other end of the line. "Ben, I think maybe you're right about his weight, but he won't tell me. And you're definitely right about his back—he's been having trouble with it for some time now. It seems to be getting worse, but he refuses to see a doctor. It's gotten so bad he can hardly even work in the garden any more. He doesn't realize that I watch him sometimes when he's out there. I see him drop to his knees in pain and come in before he really wants to. He'll never admit it though. He'll come in after ten minutes and say he's finished what he wanted to do when it's obvious he hasn't. My God, we had two-foot long zucchini growing out there this summer. Now does that sound like your father?"

Ben pictured the arched trellis laden with grapevines that led to the garden, and the straight rows and the rich, dark, weedless soil and the flawlessly healthy green plants—the garden was, he knew, his father's version of Eden, his father a kind of Prospero controlling all things good and evil. He had a sudden vivid recollection of his father insisting, as he demonstrated how to do it correctly, that there was only one right way and countless wrong ways to fold the American flag, and Ben *had better learn the right way.* Of course, his father approached everything he did that way, so for Ben the flag had simply become a metaphor for the way—according to his father, at least—you did things in life. The garden was unquestionably one of those things.

"No."

"There have been other things, too, things I'm sure he's hoping I won't pick up on, but of course I do. I don't want to embarrass him, but at the same time I'm really beginning to get concerned. He needs to see a doctor, Ben."

"What would you like *me* to do?"

"I wanted him to ask for your help with the leaves. That's why he was supposed to call you. You know how he is about getting up every last leaf before the snow comes. It's a big job, and even without the back problems it's getting to be more than the two of us can handle alone. So I told him that if he didn't call you last night, I would. Just come over with Marie and Teddy, if you want, and sort of keep an eye on him while you work. See if you agree with me. Then maybe sometime we can both approach him and convince him to have a checkup."

"Mom, I don't want to sound unwilling, but what makes you think *my* input would make any difference? You know how he is. He'll do what he wants to do no matter what anyone says—especially me."

His mother was silent at the other end of the line.

"Okay, okay. We'll be over this afternoon."

"Thank you, Ben."

"Teddy, I want you to come with me to the garden," Tom said, squatting low to speak to his grandson at eye level. "I need somebody to help me find a good pumpkin. Do you think you could do that?"

"Yes."

"Well let's go then. Tell your mom and dad you won't be gone long. Go ahead." Tom nudged his grandson forward and watched him toddle excitedly over to where his mother and father stood talking with Fran a few steps away, his fair hair glistening in the October sunlight.

"Mommy, Daddy, I won't be gone long."

"Where are you going, sweetie?" Marie said.

"Help Grampa find a pumpkin."

"What fun!"

"You help him pick out a good one, okay?" Fran said. "Grampa doesn't always pick out the good ones."

"Okay."

Tom held out his hand and Teddy ran to reach up for it with his own, his face lit with joy. "Do you want to walk or do you want me to carry you?"

"Walk!" Teddy said, and the two of them headed off toward the garden, Tom hunched over slightly to one side so that he could reach his grandson's hand.

"That looks like the long and short of it to me," Ben said, prompting a chuckle from Fran and Marie. It occurred to him, as it had so many times since Teddy was born, that he could not recall his father ever being so relaxed and easy with him. All his life, it seemed, he had felt the tension—if not the outright hostility—of unmet expectations between them, simmering always just below the surface of things, and Ben had sworn to himself when Teddy was born that he would *never* allow his father to do this again, not to *his* son. But to his surprise and confusion, it had not been an issue at all so far.

"They *are* buddies, that's for sure," Fran said. Her smile faded and her voice grew solemn. "Thank you both for coming. He would never admit it, but it will be a big help to both of us, believe me."

"Hey, a stack of papers, a pile of leaves...what's the difference?" Ben said. "At least this way Teddy can dive into the work right along with me."

The weather was clear and sunny and calm, with the sort of deep blue sky that had Ben reciting to himself, almost in reverence, as if it were a prayer, a line that he loved from Helen Hunt Jackson: "O suns and skies and clouds of June,/ And flowers of June together,/ Ye cannot rival for one hour/ October's bright blue weather." The flecks of yellow and orange and red that lay upon the ground, particularly brilliant this year and dappled by sunlight and shadow, reminded him of the vivid colors of a kaleidoscope, and he found himself wishing as he often did during the fall that there were some way to bottle and save a day like this, preserve it like an elixir, so that he could bring it forth when he needed it most and restore life, vitality, beauty to an otherwise bleak landscape. The possibility of this seemed almost real, as if the day had about it something tangible, some lustrous liquid property in the morning dew that had emanated outward as the sun rose and made everything clearer, brighter, more sharply defined—from the smallest twigs on the trees, to the blue of the river in the distance, to the colorful leaves and green blades of grass on the ground, to the azure sky itself—something that could be distilled, perhaps at nightfall, into a sort of golden essence like honey or nectar. The bees were out in force, after all—wasn't that what *they* were doing? Gathering and saving? The day was a gift, a kind of currency, he believed, meant for him and every other able-bodied person to spend outside raking leaves or cutting wood or picking apples or climbing a mountain, warm in the sunshine and cool in the shade, with only the slightest hint of winter in the faint chill breeze in the shadows, and as he worked he felt that all too rare sense of contentment, and along with it gratitude, that he was exactly where he should be, doing exactly what he should be doing.

Which was ironic, really. Although awash in leaves, the area to be raked did not seem to him now especially large, perhaps no more than half an acre altogether, but as a child it had seemed to him overwhelming. The trees, mostly maples, many of them three feet or more in diameter, towering above wide-crowned and massive, were ancient to him now, venerable, but as a boy they had been traitorous—the branches that provided such thrilling opportunies to climb or to build forts and the leaves that offered such cool shelter in the heat of summer bequeathed blisters and daunting hours of work in the fall, and despite all the pleasure he took diving and rolling and burying himself in the piles of leaves he created, he despised all the battles with his father over doing the actual work of raking and bagging, and of defining what constituted a "thorough job" and "good work." He realized, in retrospect, that his father and mother did *most* of the work while he had most of the fun, but the battles and the sense of being overwhelmed were real, and to this day he carried with him into adulthood a small reservoir of resentment toward his father for it. He wondered if his father had any sense of this at all, or his mother either for that matter, since it was she who had asked him over to help. He decided they probably did not, and that was just as well. He would make the gift of this day his gift to them, and if they knew nothing of it, so what? All the better.

He and Marie raked side by side for a time, catapulting leaves at each other with their rakes and laughing as though they were newlyweds, as though the enormous quantity of leaves all around them were not a prodigious object of labor so much as a limitless source of pleasure, an aphrodisiac if they had been alone. Marie came over to him once with her hands cupped full of crushed up dry leaves, held them beneath his nose, and said, "Smell this. Isn't this the most wonderful smell in the world? It's so *sensual*. Every time I smell this it takes me back to childhood when we used to be able to burn *huge* piles of leaves. Of course, some people probably got terrible cases of poison ivy from the smoke, but I absolutely loved it. To this day the smell of burning leaves is haunting to me—if I catch even the slightest whiff of burning leaves I get transported back to those days *immediately*. I'm a kid again, right away. Fires and Halloween and trick or treat and candy and frozen puddles on the ground with wafer thin layers of ice to stomp on and crackle open in the morning on the walk to school. A frosty walk, I might add, when you could see your breath." As if to emphasize the point she blew the handful of crushed leaves into his face, and he tackled her, laughing, into a pile they had raked. The leaves were mostly dry and brittle, but underneath they were damp and smelled of something more substantial, something hearty and musty that made him think of decay and death but also of fertility and made him want to make love to Marie right there. But his mother was raking in another corner of the yard and kept them in check ("This is supposed to be work," she called out to them, "Sounds to me like you two are having altogether too much fun over there!").

After a time—a much longer time than Ben would have expected—his father returned with Teddy, each carrying a pumpkin. Tom's was a little larger than a basketball, Teddy's about half that size.

"Looks like you did a good job helping Grampa, Teddy. You got two beautiful pumpkins," Fran said.

"I couldn't have done it without him," Tom said. "Teddy made sure I got the two best ones."

"Grampa wanted *little* ones, but I didn't," Teddy explained proudly.

"We had to do some bargaining," Tom said with a wink and a nod. "But I think we've got enough for a pie and a jack-o-lantern here. Right, Grammy?" Quite apart from the pleasure he took in growing pumpkins for his grandson and for neighboring children, Tom loved Fran's pumpkin pie.

"Oh yes, we do. I'll need some help, though. Do you think you could help me too, Teddy, or are you all tired out?"

"I'm not tired, Grammy!" Teddy bolted ahead and plunged into a pile of leaves taller than he was, rolling and flopping about and tossing leaves in the air as if he were frolicking in a pool of water. "See?" It was such a spontaneous and riveting action, such a natural thing to do, that Ben felt almost as though he were doing it himself, and it took a moment for him to understand the years of separation between himself and his son.

"I see! Good for you! Come on, now, why don't you come with me? Do you want to make a happy face or a scary face on your pumpkin?"

"Scary!"

"Okay, let's go!" Fran held out her arms and scooped her grandson up as he ran into them, picked off the leaves that clung to his hair and shirt. "See you later everybody," she said, and then whispered into Teddy's ear as they headed back toward the house.

"Don't work too hard!" Teddy called back, giggling and waving conspiratorially with his grandmother before they disappeared into the house.

"I thought you two would have been all done by now," Tom said, gazing around at the areas already gathered into mounds of leaves and the much larger areas as yet untouched by a rake. "What's the holdup?"

"We didn't want to deprive you of all this pleasure," Ben said with a sweeping, magnanimous gesture. "We know how much joy there is for you in this rite of fall." Leaves were occasionally drifting down now from the mostly bare maples above, and he realized that the breeze had begun to pick up, rustling the leaves on the ground.

"Nice of you to be so considerate."

"Any time."

"Actually," Marie interjected with a laugh, sensing an undercurrent she did not quite trust, "I think Fran gathered up most of these piles. Ben and I got a little sidetracked at times."

"Ben has a history of that when it comes to raking leaves, so don't take it personally. Right, Ben?"

Ben was silent, and Marie finally said, "Well, if we don't get going here we won't finish before winter, never mind by the end of this afternoon."

She did not know how prophetic her words would turn out to be. As the afternoon wore on the breeze became a swirling, gusting wind that made their task far more difficult, all the more so because early on Tom was forced to quit. They saw him crumple almost to his knees once without uttering a sound, though neither one said anything to him then, but it wasn't long afterwards when his back began to ache so severely that he could barely remain standing.

"I'm sorry," he said, "but I'm going to have to stop. Just leave the rest of this for another day." Without even waiting for an answer he turned and hobbled slowly toward the house, his right arm bent behind him with his hand pressing against his low back.

He's like an old man, Ben thought. "We'll just finish up here and be in later."

His father did not turn around. "Suit yourself," he said, with a dismissive wave of his left hand. "Thanks."

"It's amazing," Ben said to Marie as they watched him limp his way back to the house and disappear within. "I never would have believed I'd see the day."

"What do you think it is?"

"I don't know, but one way or another we're going to find out."

They worked together raking and bagging for the rest of the afternoon, fighting the wind every step of the way, their earlier mood of playfulness and frivolity replaced by a serious, workmanlike determination to get the job done. Except for a brief interlude when Fran brought them some cider and zucchini bread (Teddy was napping), they pressed on until the light began to fade and the wind died down. When Fran finally called them to come in for dinner, they were just finishing up. Darkness had come on quickly and it was growing colder. They hadn't seen Tom in hours.

Tom joined them for dinner, though his face looked drawn in the muted dining room light, dimmed in deference to Teddy's jack-o-lantern, which served as the centerpiece of the table. He did not speak much. He had taken three ibuprofen and spent most of the time since he had left them lying down, which had given him a small measure of relief. It was obvious to those around him though that he found it difficult to sit at the dinner table. Except for a brief exchange with Teddy over what he planned to be for Halloween ("A skeleton that glows in the dark!" he told Fran), conversation was desultory and subdued. Without anyone openly suggesting it, they all hurried through the meal and the much-anticipated pumpkin pie. Afterwards, Marie set Teddy up in the TV room with the Disney Channel and returned to help clear away the dishes.

Ben took a sip of his coffee. He was the only one to have coffee with his pie, although Marie and his mother were drinking tea. His father had declined even the pie. "So what's going on with your back, old man?" Ben asked.

Tom did not answer right away. "It's nothing. I think I've told you this before, arthritis flares up every once in a while. Today was a little worse than usual, that's all."

"How do you know it's arthritis?"

"Because it's what happens to people who've lived as long as I have and worked the kind of jobs I've worked."

"When did you get your degree?"

"What?"

"Your medical degree."

There was a long uneasy silence. Ben gazed at his father with a kind of ruthless intensity. "Have you seen a doctor yet?"

"No."

"Why not?" His father did not respond, kept his eyes lowered. Ben continued as if he were chasing down an elusive prey almost within reach. "You're afraid, aren't you? That's what is really going on here. You're afraid."

"Ben..." Marie started.

"No, let him answer."

But there was no reply, and the glow from Teddy's jack-o-lantern flickered soundlessly at the center of the table. At last Fran said, softly, "Tom, you have to admit you haven't been feeling up to par for some time now. And it's not just your back I'm talking about."

Tom gazed impassively at each of them for a long moment, then rose slowly from the table and left the room without saying a word.

"Tom...?" Fran called after him, "Honey?" but he continued on down the hallway without turning around. "I'm sorry," she said, glancing from Ben to Marie with a crestfallen look. "I didn't mean for you two to get so caught in the middle. But I don't know what to do. You can see how he is—he refuses to listen about seeing a doctor, yet he's in pain now every day. He's stopped running—hasn't been out in weeks—and he's not sleeping well. He can't make it through a single night without having to get up at least two or three times to go to the bathroom." She shook her head in confusion. "I'm just very worried."

Marie reached over and placed her hand on Fran's. "He'll come around, I think," Marie said.

"I'm sorry if I've made things worse, Mom," Ben said.

"It couldn't be worse than your father doing nothing about it. Please, don't feel bad. You two have done a lot for him today, and he knows it, and that's probably where some of his frustration is coming from. He's a stubborn old yankee who wants to do everything by himself, and when he can't, he doesn't like it."

In the silence that followed they could hear the sounds of Teddy's laughter coming from the TV room. "Let's just hope Marie is right. Let's just hope he'll come around."

He could hear the faint scratching and soft clawed footsteps of a mouse tunneling about somewhere inside a wall near him, but except for this it was quiet and dark in the bedroom where he lay on his back, listening but far enough away that he could no longer hear the others, a welcoming quiet and darkness in which he could sift through his own expectations as well as those of others and confront what was most important without masks or pretenses. He knew that Fran was right to urge him to see a doctor, and that she was acting today out of desperation and love because he had given her no alternative, no honest acknowledgement, in her more private pleas to him. And he knew that he would, in time, abide by her wishes. He loved her more than he loved his own pride. He knew also that he had heard something in the wind and the rustling leaves and his grandson's peals of joy that frightened him. He could admit that now here in the quiet and the darkness, in the solitude and separateness. He was not yet sure what it was that he had heard, although it had something powerful and irresistible about it, some indefinable force that was calling him away from what he knew, drawing him toward itself as inexorably as the tide drew all things in to shore or out to sea. Ben had sensed this, although Ben had assumed it was the doctor he feared, or perhaps death, and of course this was true too, but it was something more also, something which he could hear but not yet understand.

Chapter Three

Art and Artifice

When Tom awoke that night the moon was full and clear and the bedroom was bathed in silver light, though it was not the moonlight that woke him. It was the pain in his bones and the urge to urinate, which was so strong that he was forced to get up and go to the bathroom. It happened to him more than once now every night, and sometimes, like tonight, he was not able to get back to sleep. Tonight as always he rolled the covers back and tried to slip quietly, surreptitiously out of bed—which was not easy due to the pain—in hopes of not waking Fran, but he knew right away that it was pointless to return to bed. The moon was too bright, the pain too strong, his thoughts too insistent for any easy slide back into bed and sleep, so after a brief trip to the bathroom he made his way to the couch in the study and lay there trying not to move, thinking and remembering and longing for sleep.

He remembered Ben as a newborn lying on his back in the sunlight, awash in the slanting golden rays of a July morning, shirtless and scrawny and slightly jaundiced, breathing softly, arms drawn up and folded with hands behind his head in blissful, unsuspecting repose, and he remembered how often at night in the silence and darkness he would go over to the crib to watch and listen for his infant son's breathing, and if he could not readily see or hear what he needed to and even sometimes when he could he would

[25]

reach down to the tiny sleeping figure and place his hand gently on his son's back—his hand enormous against such a diminutive form—to feel reassurance in the soft rise and fall of what meant life to him, his son's life and his own life, not just life in its most primitive sense of lungs taking in oxygen, and not just in that connection of himself to all the generations that might follow and so signify the continuation of something enduring and perhaps even eternal, nor even life in the bridge that he himself provided between his son and his own father and thus to all the generations that preceded them, but life in the sense of all that was meaningful and good, life in the sense of bounty and prosperity and limitless potential, life in the sense of a beating heart that engendered all the promise of joy and danger and threat and loss and hope that existence could possibly offer. And he remembered also how in the years that followed, the early years, Ben would awake sometimes in the middle of the night and crawl into bed between him and Fran and snuggle himself there, at once a wedge between them and a bond that joined them, his breath sweet and his body small, a miniature furnace pumping out warmth and radiating security, the guileless unfeigned security of a sleeping child who has no reason yet nor has developed any capacity yet to conceive of anything else, and how Ben would awake again later when it was light outside, sleepy-eyed and distant at first as though he were coming to them from a world far away and alien, but then soon enough bright-eyed and smiling and wriggling about, an uncontainable concentration of raw energy and laughter, life instantly a game of something: of hide 'n seek beneath the covers; of startling, fearful discovery—"Oh my, Tom! There's a mouse in our bed!"; of fishing for trout but catching only a small "bony pickerel" that thrashed about and must be tossed unceremoniously back into the water, so bony that if eaten he must be spat out: "pitouey"; life instantly charged with the urge to move, the unconscious urge to move—electric, irrepressible, all-consuming—the direction unimportant so long as there was movement, the day unconsidered and yet brimming with possibility, infinite possibility because there was no end in sight, and no end in sight because time did not exist, there was no such thing as time, only movement and sensation and the desire to keep on moving, life's instinctive impetus and most sacred precept—infused in his son, embodied by his son, indistinguishable from and most purely in harmony with choice and will, more purely than it would ever be again: to live meant to move and to move meant to live, nothing more, nothing else, each moment new and fresh and joyful, lived without regret or sorrow in the present because the past had not yet been born.

He remembered how tired he would feel in the days immediately after Ben was born, and how he would sometimes allow himself a nap in the middle of the afternoon, deliberately recalling the entire day of Ben's birth as a kind of mantra, a sedative and tragi-comic three-part litany beginning with the antic (in retrospect only) hurried drive to the hospital on that steamy mid-July morning and the recognition there that a new life was not just imminent but coming on much faster and more violently than either he or Fran had ever anticipated, and then followed by the harrowing decision to do an immediate cesarean—he would never forget how quickly the blood and the pain on her face and in her breathing unmanned him, humbled him, transforming his unbridled excitement into fear and a sense of being useless to her, irrelevant, he the "coach" and comforter pathetically in need of comfort himself—and then the abrupt entrance (which he did not see) into the world of their child, pink and frail and with flecks of blood still on him, his face contorted, a boy, a son! and then concluding at last with the moments of holding him, all three together, he and Fran and now Ben together, and the feeling of bliss so total, so utterly complete in his heart that he wanted to sing out: O, my son! O, my son! Here is my son!—and so recalling it all, smiling, buoyant, filled with a transcendent inner calm and the unshakeable belief that everything, everything, was right with the world—his son was born, all was possible, all was well—now he could sleep, now he could drift gently, safely into sleep.

He remembered how Ben at only four or five years old showed an astonishing talent for drawing, sitting down sometimes for hours with only a pencil and crayons or markers and calling upon his imagination and his extraordinary capacity to study an object—to observe it carefully and render its details with a patience far beyond his age—to produce work that he as an adult, as an architect himself, could only marvel at. He loved to watch his son at such moments, wondered with a kind of humility and awe if there were not some of himself, some of his own predilection toward visual expression and exacting standards of precision, in these artistic sallies, dreamed of his son's future as an artist, a painter perhaps, and proudly imagined his son's work hanging on his walls and in galleries. Yet Ben was more disorganized and more demanding than he himself had ever been, possessed confounding Midas-like abilities: on the one hand to turn whatever he touched into chaos— his room, the play room, any area where he worked or played, leaving clothes, toys, tools behind him as though after he used them they no longer existed despite all the messy evidence to the contrary—while on the other hand to turn a blank piece of paper into a thing of beauty through painstaking toil and a frightening degree of perfectionism, a perfectionism so unremitting that Ben could more easily throw hours worth of his work in the trash than spend time looking at it or showing it to others. He did not ever want to subvert Ben's authority over his own efforts, but he found it difficult to see Ben cast aside fine work, to bear silent witness to his son's harsh final judgments, and once, only once—after he had asked Ben why he was throwing the picture away and been told, "Because it's not a beautiful one. If it's not a beautiful one, I throw it away"—when he could not convince Ben of its worth and absolutely could not abide the thought that it would be lost forever, he pilfered from the trash a picture Ben had sketched of a loon in profile upon the water, replete with the delicate black and white latticework of its feathers, black head and long pointed black beak tilted slightly upward, the small red bead of its eye gazing above as if yearning for the freedom of the sky while somehow trapped below. Ben was not quite four at the time, and by five and a half or six years old—in a crushing disappointment to him that Ben could not possibly have intended or understood—Ben no longer drew at all, so frustrated was he by his inability to represent subjects with the realism and exactness he demanded of himself.

He longed for Ben to know of these memories which were the signatures of his heart, these moments, these impressions, these nuances of thought and feeling which were imprinted indelibly there upon his heart, his very being, identifying him more accurately than a set of fingerprints and defining him more truly, more profoundly than any DNA profile ever could, but Ben did not know any of this, had no way of knowing any of this, and therein lay a great mystery he had never quite been able to fathom in his life: why he could not speak to his son in terms—in words—that came from his heart, why he could not explain to Ben what he felt most deeply. Could he never find the right words to say what he meant—was he so inarticulate? Was he afraid that what he might say would sound foolish, even sentimental to his son, and embarrass both of them? Did he fear that the power of what he felt would somehow be diminished or cheapened by words, that only actions could speak to what was inside him? Or was he simply afraid, period, just another coward hiding behind age-old taboos against a man revealing what was inside him? In the end, always, he would not say what he wanted, what he meant, the words would choke in his throat, or come out in twisted form as some petty complaint—"Why don't you clean your room, it's disgusting," he would say, standing in Ben's doorway when Ben was a teenager, in lieu of the simple "Good night" and "I love you" that he felt; or instead of recognizing his *relief that Ben had returned home safely after driving on a long trip, perhaps a ski trip with friends, he might greet Ben with, "Welcome home. I'm sure I can expect to see the gas tank full"—and in the accumulation of years such warped transmissions developed their own weight and history, and it became easier and easier to deliver them upon first impulse—the ruses, the deceptions, the red herrings of sarcasm—and nearly impossible to unearth and speak what was beneath them. He* knew *what was beneath them but not in the moments he spoke, only afterwards upon reflection, upon remembering—and even that, remembering, had grown blurred— that there had been a time when Ben was young when he used to say "I love you" to his son without any self-consciousness, when "my sweet boy" or "my sweet son" or "Benny-boy" or "Benj-of-mine" would roll off his tongue without the slightest hesitation or sense of awkwardness. When it all ceased and why he could not recall any longer, only that it had ceased, and that what had once seemed so natural and easy to him had now taken on the quality of myth. What he had wanted to do in that time long ago was sing to his son, herald his life and worth to the world, but what he had come to do as a matter of course and as a way of life was to criticize and admonish, and the thought that he had undermined his son and betrayed himself, had denied what was purest in his heart and had wasted years of opportunity saddened him beyond measure.*

And the sadness seemed to feed the pain, which he could feel throbbing deep inside him even as he lay there in the silver moonlight trying to remain motionless, throbbing in the low bones of his back and in his hips and in the upper bones of his thighs— the throb of something evil, some malevolent force that had caused him several weeks ago to give up his nearly lifelong habit of running and that seemed not to be attacking from the outside and driving itself inward against his defenses, not an invader, but an enemy of even darker origin, a force emanating from within the core of his being and driving outward, relentlessly outward, as if to expel him from himself. A cry, a moan escaped his lips and he noted it with surprise, and then Fran (dear Fran!) *was near him although he did not know when or how she had arrived or even if she were real, and she was saying something to him in a soft voice, whispery and tender, about how he could not go on this way, about how she loved him and would suffer with him through whatever lay ahead but she would not allow him to go on this way, and as he felt her cradling him against her body he could also feel himself nodding his agreement and thinking,* there, it's outside of me now.

Tom hadn't seen Dr. Marshall, his own doctor, in three or four years, since the plantar fasciitis problem that had sidelined him from running for a few months. Dr. Marshall had told him at the time that he ought to be having a complete physical exam annually at his age, not just showing up when things broke down, especially given his family history of both his father and grandfather dying of heart attacks before reaching age sixty-five. He hadn't followed the doctor's advice, although it was not because he disliked Dr. Marshall or distrusted his opinion. On the contrary, he had always found Dr. Marshall a likeable and straight-shooting kind of man, a man he could respect. It was more that he didn't feel the need for the intrusive poking and prodding of an annual exam because he had been keeping himself fit all his life through running, watching his diet while still eating well, taking low-strength aspirin daily since he had turned forty-five, having his cholesterol screened on a regular basis, and generally taking what he considered a proactive approach to his health. And it had worked. He had rarely been sick in his life, when he had been it was never serious, and he had *never* been hospitalized, not even for one day. If he were going to have a heart attack, there was not much more he could do to prevent it. What would happen would happen, annual physical or no annual physical.

The back problem was nothing new—his back had been bothering him for years, and he had already been to see a number of doctors and chiropractors about it (he had even considered going to an acupuncturist, but he could never quite bring himself to that point). No one had ever been able to relieve the discomfort more than temporarily or to give him any definitive answers about its cause, and over time he had come to accept the problems with his back as a condition of his life. He had also assumed, trying to be realistic about it, that there was a great probability of developing arthritis as he grew older, so it did not surprise him when he began to feel, intermittently and infrequently at first, a sharper and more intense kind of pain. He had been expecting it, in a way. What he had not been expecting was that it would continue to get worse, and that it would incapacitate him to the point that it had in recent months.

"Tom, I'd like to see you again soon," Dr. Marshall said after he had completed the exam and Tom had finished dressing. "I'll skip all the lectures and just ask you a simple question. When was the last time you had your prostate examined?"

Tom furrowed his brow and thought about it. "I don't know. Years ago, I guess. I don't remember."

Dr. Marshall nodded. "That's pretty much what I expected. I knew you hadn't had an exam with me in the last few years, but I wondered if maybe you had been to see anyone else." His tone was non-judgemental but his expression was serious. "I don't want to alarm you, but I didn't like what I felt when I examined your prostate. It felt much larger and harder than it should. It's typical for someone your age to have an enlarged prostate, but this went well beyond what would be typical. Which could mean more than one thing, of course, especially considering the urinary problems you say you've been having. But given what I felt and what you've described about your back pains, I don't want to take any chances. I'll know more tomorrow when I get the results of your PSA test, but I'd like to run some other tests as soon as possible."

I knew I shouldn't have come here, Tom thought, feeling as if he had just been asked a question in a language he did not understand. The question was meant for someone else, someone who spoke the language. "Other than a public service announcement, what's a PSA?"

Dr. Marshall gave a faint smile. "It stands for prostate-specific antigen, which is an enzyme manufactured by the prostate. The important thing is that the level of your PSA can be measured by analyzing a small sample of your blood. In someone your age, what we'd like to see is a measurement of less than four. Preferably even lower."

"What if it's higher than that?"

"Well, that would all depend on *how* much higher it is." The doctor gazed at Tom with a steadfast expression. "I don't want to be disingenuous about this, Tom. What we're concerned about here is the possibility of prostate cancer. Above age fifty it happens to men far more often than most people know. It happens more often than breast cancer in women, but we just don't hear about it anywhere near as much."

"I've known other men that have had prostate cancer," Tom said, possessed by a peculiar sense that he was standing somewhere above and outside of his body, listening in on this conversation between himself and Dr. Marshall with a sort of detached fascination. "But to be honest, I never really even considered that *I* might have it."

"It's a possibility, Tom, but let's not jump to that conclusion. As I said, we'll know more tomorrow, and we'll schedule other tests that will definitely give us more information. In the meantime, I'm glad you came in when you did. Just try not to worry too much. Go home and have a glass of wine with your wife and try to relax."

Easy for you to say. "I'll try. Thanks."

Fran had come with him and was sitting in the waiting room flipping through a magazine when he came out. She gave him a questioning look but did not say anything until they were outside in the car. "So what did Dr. Marshall have to say?"

Tom started up the ignition and began to drive away before answering. "He didn't like what he felt when he examined my prostate. He'll know more tomorrow when he gets the results of something called a PSA test, but he wants me to go back as soon as possible for more tests."

They were both silent for a moment until Tom said, "I thought I'd finished all this test taking years ago with the SAT's and the GRE's, but I guess there's no end to taking tests in life—now I've got the PSA and God knows what other tests to pass."

Fran smiled, then reached over and gently stroked his thigh. "What was it he didn't like about your prostate?"

Tom was looking at the wild get-ups of the young rebels hanging out on the corner in front of the North Church as they drove past. He had been living in Portsmouth now for more than thirty-five years, and he had seen the guises come and go on the perpetually young habitues of this local hangout. The "hippie" look had persisted for many years, with the long hair and patched jeans and vests and beads and bandannas of all kinds, but in time it had given way to other looks involving either no hair—the skinhead look—or colored hair: pink, purple, orange, the wilder the better, sometimes spiked front to back like a Mohawk-style Statue of Liberty, black leather clothing and shiny metal chains, and most recently pierced lips, eyebrows, noses—whatever *could* be pierced—and tattoos of all shapes, sizes, and colors on all parts of the body, from small butterflies and ladybugs on the ankle to sharply pointed lines and arabesques bisecting the upper arm like seismograph readings. Every time he walked or drove past he found it ironic and mildly amusing (he was sure the young denizens of the corner would find his amusement condescending, but he meant no harm) to reflect upon the truism that try as each generation might to establish its own essential identity, to break with the past by creating personas and styles shockingly different from those of its predecessors, the more the essence of the place, this little corner of non-conformism in Portsmouth, remained constant and unchanging. And by extension, the more each generation affirmed its connection to the past, to that vast panoply of costumes and fashions throughout history that signified human life.

"He said it felt too large and too hard."

"What does that mean?"

"I don't know. He said it could mean many things, which was why he wanted to get more information. I didn't ask what the *many things* might be."

Fran was growing mildly agitated. "Is that all? He didn't even tell you what the main possibilities are?"

Tom thought about what to say but found he could not give an answer, and for a long moment the question hung there between them. It was one thing to be sitting in a doctor's examination room discussing cancer with the sort of clinical objectivity and detachment that the context seemed to require, but it was quite another thing to speak the word to his wife sitting here in the quiet confines of their car. At last he said, "He talked about the possibility of prostate cancer, but he didn't want me to assume that's what it is."

In speaking the word he felt as though he had just crossed a line that placed him—*them*—in altogether new territory, and even without glancing over he could feel Fran's unwavering gaze upon him.

"What else might it be?" she asked in a softer, less agitated voice than before.

He could feel her sizing him up, searching his demeanor to see if he was being totally honest with her. "I don't know. He didn't say, and I didn't ask."

"So he talked about prostate cancer but nothing else? He didn't talk about any other possibilities...and you didn't ask him?"

"That's right," Tom said, feeling with sudden acuteness the inadequacy of his answers. He had known even at the time that he should have asked more of Dr. Marshall, probed further into the meaning of "well beyond what would be typical," but he had felt disinclined then, just as he did now, to go too far down any unknown road. His only serious question had led them to talk about prostate cancer, and that was plenty far enough for him.

"Well it's pretty obvious, my dear Thomas, that the next time you visit Dr. Marshall I'm going to have to be there with you." Fran patted him on his thigh with the soft, light touch she might use on a newborn's back.

That's all right by me, he thought in some secret, terrified part of his being, *because I don't want to be there alone,* but he did not offer a reply. He kept his gaze fixed on the road ahead as they continued to weave their way through the narrow streets of Portsmouth and drove past the Piscataqua River, where he noticed a cormorant sitting dark and still upon the surface of the water before it suddenly plunged its long beak into the river's swirling currents and disappeared.

Chapter Four

The Gales of November

It was Dr. Marshall himself who called Tom the next day to discuss the results of the PSA test. When he realized who it was, Tom thought of calling out to Fran so that she could pick up on another phone, but he decided against it on an impulse he could not have explained to himself, let alone to her. He knew she was due to head out soon to work as a volunteer at a local blood drive, as she often did, and he did not want to delay her, but although this was a reason for his silence he knew it was not the only reason. Instead of calling out, he cradled the phone closer to himself like a man having an affair and moved out of earshot from her.

He received the news from the doctor that his PSA results were "not encouraging" with an equanimity he found surprising, even in that detached, analytical portion of his brain that had served him so well as an architect over the years. As he listened to the doctor explain what the number was, and how that number was far higher than it should be, and how important it was for Tom to schedule further testing right away, and how he would like to meet with Tom as soon as possible to discuss the situation in more detail, he found himself nodding politely as if the doctor were right there in the room with him and he were merely acknowledging information he had already heard before. He moved back toward the kitchen where Fran was announcing that she was about to leave, smiled and waved to her as she puckered her lips, blew him a kiss, and walked out the door, and assured the doctor he would meet with him whenever the doctor wanted.

"Four o'clock today would be fine," Tom said. "I'll be there."

He knew there was a disconnect between his response and the words he was hearing that would disappear sooner or later, leaving him to deal with emotions he could not yet feel. But for now, it surprised him simply that he was not surprised. He took in the doctor's words uncritically, as he would any factual explanation of basic physical laws, and did not ask questions. The doctor might as well have been explaining the principles of gravity to him.

At the moment, he was experiencing no pain in his back and there were no obligations to weigh him down, nothing he absolutely had to do, so he decided to take a walk outside on a path along the river where he often used to run. November had come in, as it seemed it always did, gray and bleak, and today was no different, although he was thankful that for now at least there was no wind. November and wind inevitably reminded him of when he and Fran used to listen to a singer named Gordon Lightfoot, whose ballad "The Wreck of the Edmund Fitzgerald" told a story of how "the gales of November came early" one year and doomed the venerable ship and all its crew in a terrible storm somewhere out on Lake Superior. Powerful and sad, the song had always served to define his feelings about the month. It was the wind, in part, that made him think of November as the hardest month of the year—the wind and the barren black trees and the deepening frost and the diminishing light, darkness consuming more of every day with such relentless force that on particularly raw gray days it seemed to him the sun never rose, and what little light there was appeared as feeble and spiritless as the twilight of an Arctic winter. Only hardwoods like oaks and hickories held onto any of their leaves at this time of year, but the leaves were brown and brittle and shriveled, clinging to their branches by the slightest of threads with a kind of grim and pathetic stubbornness.

As he ambled slowly along the worn path he could hear crows cawing to each other in the distance somewhere across the river. Shrill squawks drew his attention to a pair of blue jays flitting from branch to branch in a black cherry tree nearby, pecking at some sort of small dark hanging masses. The jays flew off when he walked over for a closer inspection and discovered what they were pecking at: the shrunken remains of caterpillar webs that appeared without fail—randomly and overnight, it seemed—at the end of every summer, blighting trees for a couple of months with their ugly gray clouds. The jays must have been after dead caterpillars trapped inside the decaying webs.

Farther along he reached an area where the river came very close to a well-traveled road. Cars occasionally whizzed past behind him as he stood for a moment and looked around. Here there appeared to be no current at all, and the placid surface of the river was an oily black where it reflected the far shore, a sort of opaque gray-white that mirrored the sky on his side. Mixed in among the oaks and pines were numerous dead elms, some whose massive trunks had broken off long ago and left behind outsized stumps fifteen or twenty feet tall, some whose once graceful, slender branches remained, though pockmarked now by woodpeckers and broken off at angles that made them look like gnarled claws reaching toward the sky. In the tangles of low, rust-colored brush all about him lay the waste of humanity: stryrofoam coffee cups and worm containers and plastic soda bottles and empty cigarette packages and beer cans and multifarious layers of paper and cardboard from Burger King and McDonald's—convenience items, mostly, but there were larger items too such as a stained mattress and a rusted twenty-gallon propane tank. Near the river's edge were a few bird's nests of monofilament fishing line that he picked up and deposited in his pocket for fear that some small creature might get trapped in one of them. Suspended inexplicably from a dead branch that arched over the river was a dark cord that hung down to the water, and dangling from that were more strands of monofilament line and bobbers and treble-hooked lures. In counterpoint to the waste and disorder surrounding him, he saw as he gazed out beyond it all that the river possessed a tranquil beauty which remained undiminished, and although he had run past this area many times before, he noticed for the first time a white pine tree standing very tall on a spit of land on the opposite shore. The tree was dead, its black branches entirely devoid of anything green, and yet the branches spread away from the trunk intact on either side in a kind of marvelous symmetry, very wide at the base near the ground and narrowing proportionately all the way to the spire at the top. Then he realized that the symmetry extended into the river, where the slightly darker mirror image of the tree upon the surface reached in perfect alignment all the way across, its spire pointing not toward the ambiguous gray sky but toward his side of the river, toward him.

Tom arrived at the doctor's office promptly by four o'clock but had to wait nearly an hour to see Dr. Marshall. He had expected there would be a backlog and he would have to wait given that it was the end of the day, but as he watched the door to the waiting room open time after time and admit ahead of him even those who had arrived after him, and as the pain in his back grew more acute (it had started bothering him again shortly after his walk and he had almost called to cancel the appointment), his patience began to wear thin—waiting was a part of the doctor visit game that he had no use for. Other professional people with important work to do scheduled appointments with clients and managed to be on time, so why couldn't doctors? If in his professional life as an architect he had kept people waiting the way doctors routinely did, he would have been out of work in short order. *They know you can't do without them, and they make sure you know it too,* he thought angrily.

"Mr. Derringer?" It was the young, overweight woman who had been opening the door and escorting people to the inner recesses of the office. He was the only one left in the waiting room.

"Yes," he said, nodding politely and following her through the maze of halls and doorways behind the door. She led him to a small room furnished with an orange vinyl arm chair and a black examination table covered with paper.

"The doctor will be with you in just a moment."

"Thank you," he said, as she closed the door behind her. He wondered why it seemed such a disproportionate number of people working in health professions were overweight and out of shape, and then he felt a pang of remorse because he knew it was not the young woman's fault that he had had to wait so long.

After at least another five minutes of waiting in this room (which he assumed must be standard procedure, since there were magazines here too) he heard the rustling of papers outside the door and Dr. Marshall entered.

"Tom," the doctor said, looking him straight in the eye and extending his hand for a handshake, "I'm glad you could come in today. It's important that we get to work on this situation right away."

"Thanks for seeing me so quickly."

Dr. Marshall nodded. "As I mentioned to you on the phone, your PSA number is very troubling, especially given what I felt during the examination and what you've said about your urinary problems and your back pains."

"You don't think the back pains could be arthritis?"

"That's always a possibility," Dr. Marshall said, though it was clear he did not believe this. "But right now we need to get more information before we can draw any conclusions. The first thing we need to do is a biopsy to find out whether or not there's anything malignant in your prostate. I don't want to rule anything in or out until we get that information, so I'd like to order a biopsy for you right away."

It was not a question, exactly, but Tom understood that the doctor was looking for his permission. "How soon is right away?"

"Within the next two or three days. I'd also like to have some x-rays taken. That could be done tonight or tomorrow."

Tom thought about this. "You're not wasting any time."

"Tom, I want to find out what's going on with you. The sooner we get more information, the sooner we'll know—or at least have a better idea of—what the problem is. Then we can begin to deal with that problem." He paused for a moment to emphasize what he was about to say. "Now is not a time to move slowly—there's too much at stake here."

Dr. Marshall leaned back against the countertop and gazed steadily at Tom as he let the words sink in. His hands were folded and resting upon his midsection in a pose of patient expectation.

"Let me see if I'm understanding this correctly," Tom said in genuine confusion. "I don't mean to sound like I'm questioning you, but on the one hand you say you don't know yet what my problem is, and on the other hand you're telling me it's important that we act immediately. Isn't there some sort of a contradiction here?"

Dr. Marshall took a deep breath and pursed his lips, though his gaze remained fixed and his hands never moved. "The odds very much point to the possibility of cancer based on what we already know, but it's not a certainty yet. We need to find out if, in fact, there is cancer, and if there is, where it's located and what type it is. That's why there is definitely some urgency involved. There's still a slight possibility it could be something else— benign prostatic hyperplasia, or BPH, for example, could certainly be causing the urinary problems you've been having and could, in rare cases, account for the high PSA level you're showing. BPH is present at least to some degree in most men your age. But given all the evidence we have so far, the most prudent thing for us to do now is get the biopsy done."

Biopsy. PSA. BPH. Is this all a bad joke? Tom shifted in his chair and winced from the pain in his back as he moved. The doctor's eyes narrowed. "What's BPH?" he said, latching onto this new possibility no matter how absurd or exotic its name might sound. The meaning of the simple word *cancer* was beginning to grow all too real and clear.

"It's a condition of prostate enlargement caused by the growth of non-cancerous cells. This growth can expand the prostate outward, which is something that can be felt in a digital rectal exam, but it can also expand inward and squeeze the urethra, which runs right through the middle of the prostate, and this can't be felt. Think of the urethra as sort of like a garden hose being squeezed in the middle while you're trying to run water through it. That's what BPH is like, and that's why it creates so many difficulties with urination. It generally gets worse over time, but it might take years of gradually increasing difficulties with urination before the problem becomes acute.

And as I said, BPH *can* increase a man's PSA level, though not usually so high as yours is."

But it is possible, Tom thought.

"However," Dr. Marshall continued, as though he had read Tom's mind, "BPH would not explain your back pain. That's what concerns me the most, and that's why I'd like to have you get x-rays taken as soon as possible. Preferably when you leave here, if you can."

Rising up inside him was a kind of rebellion, and Tom could feel himself wanting to object to something that he could not yet articulate. "What about the biopsy? What's involved in that?"

"It's a pretty simple procedure, really," the doctor said reassuringly. He continued to lean against the counter behind him in a relaxed manner but his hands grew animated as he began to explain. "It's painless, there's no anesthesia involved, and it doesn't take very long. A device that uses ultrasound will be inserted into your rectum and will guide a very thin needle into areas of your prostate that look suspicious. A tiny sample of tissue will be taken from each of these areas, possibly several different areas, and from these a pathologist should be able to give us a very clear idea of whether or not there's any cancer, and if so, what type. We should have the results within two or three days afterward."

He was beginning to feel as though he didn't want to ask any more questions because he just might get answers—answers he did not want to hear. "I guess there's not much choice in the matter then, really."

"I wouldn't advise waiting, Tom, at least not now. There *are* men with prostate cancer who eventually decide to try 'watchful waiting' rather than going through surgery or radiation, but at this point we need to find out what we're dealing with before we decide on a course of treatment."

The doctor raised his eyebrows and Tom nodded his reluctant approval. "I'm writing out the order here for x-rays," Dr. Marshall said as he scribbled away on a carbon form. "When you go over to the hospital to have the x-rays taken you can also schedule a time for the biopsy."

Dr. Marshall tore off the top sheet and handed the rest of the form to him, looking him directly in the eye. "And, Tom," he added, proffering a small white square of paper, "I've also written out a prescription here for something to help you with your back pain."

Tom glanced down at the paper as he accepted it from the doctor. The handwriting was unintelligible. "Thank you."

The doctor extended his hand once again for a handshake, his left hand softly embracing Tom's upper arm. "Good luck, Tom."

Tom nodded. "Thanks."

"I'll be talking to you soon."

When he left the doctor's office it was full dark outside and he was immediately hit by a chill blast of wind, cold even for November. Sifting through the jumble of emotions he was experiencing he realized that what he felt most profoundly was a peculiar sense of betrayal. During much of his adult life he had been preparing himself for—*and expecting to face*—problems with his heart. Both his father and his father's father had died of heart attacks at a relatively early age. He was only about five years old when his grandfather died at age sixty-two, and despite possessing very few memories of the man himself, he did remember clearly his grandfather's funeral and the ride to the cemetery and standing over the open grave next to his father. In the hearse he became aware that even though his father was sitting up straight in the front seat, facing forward with his head raised and apparently gazing through the windshield, tears were coming from his eyes, and the tears continued streaming silently down his cheeks all through the service at the graveside where he stood with his head down and his chin tucked to his chest. It was the first and only time Tom had ever seen his father cry. There was never any talk of it afterward, never any explanation or stories about his grandfather to give Tom a context other than his own feelings for his father. There was merely the unforgettable fact of what he had seen. Later, at the reception held at his house, there was a feast of food and drink, greater by far than anything there had ever been in his house before, and both his father and stepmother laughed and joked and traded stories with people as if nothing bad at all had just happened, as if, on the contrary, he had only imagined his father's tears in some waking dream or fantasy, while the reality was what he saw here, a party, a celebration, his father laughing with joy.

His father must have been in his early forties at the time, because it was only about ten years later, at age fifty-two, that his father was in the grave himself after a heart attack and Tom as a fifteen year old was standing at the graveside next to his stepmother, trying to force back tears while consoling her. There was a reception and a large gathering again at his house afterward, but the tone was much more subdued—his father was loved by all who knew him, which was most everybody in the small town they lived in, and fifty-two was too young by everyone's standards. There were stories, to be sure, stories about his father's extraordinary work ethic and his generosity and his love of family, but the stories were all tinged with sadness at the inevitable realization the only reason for telling them was that Michael J. Derringer was dead, and that he was dead sooner than he should have been.

Two of the accounts Tom heard that day stood out to him for revealing aspects of his father he had never quite understood. The first gave him some explanation and insight as to why his father was gone so much of the time, particularly in the evenings. His father had worked his whole adult life for a local oil company, sometimes as a driver but more often as a furnace repairman. Tom had little doubt he enjoyed what he did, or that he was hardworking and loyal—he always had a smile when he came home, never missed a day of work due to sickness (none that Tom saw, anyway), and no matter how long he scrubbed at the kitchen sink he could not erase the network of black lines scribed into all the cracks and fissures of his callused hands. What Tom had never understood though about his father's work was why it seemed he was gone nearly *all* the time, especially in the coldest and darkest part of the year. It seemed the less daylight there was, the longer his father was absent from home.

On one unforgettable day in January when Tom was only six or seven, light snow started to fall early in the morning and intensified as the meager afternoon light gave way to darkness and the full-scale fury of a blizzard. Tom and his stepmother and his younger sister, Alice, huddled around the radio in the kitchen, listening to weather reports and hoping to see the headlights of his father's truck swing into the driveway at any moment. In the glow cast by the outside light they could see violent winds driving the snow horizontal but Tom went to bed that night not knowing what had happened to his father. He awoke the next morning to find his father had already left for work again despite snow continuing to fall heavily. His stepmother explained that the emergency calls last night and again this morning were necessary because even in such terrible weather—*especially* in such terrible weather—people still needed to have their furnaces working. They still needed to have *heat.* Tom did not truly understand the significance of her words though until he heard Mrs. McDuffee, a widow in her eighties, telling her story at the reception after the funeral. She described with such clarity the details of "a blizzard one night in January" that Tom knew exactly what night she was talking about. Her furnace had gone dead and she was "quite terrified" that she would freeze to death until "there was Michael coming to my home like a Godsend." She said he came in "with snow on his hair and a smile on his face," and he left, after fixing her furnace and sitting with her for a few moments to have a cup of coffee and a piece of pie, "with a smudge of black grease on his forehead and a smile still on his face." He was, she said, "the archangel himself" to her that night, and altogether "a wonderful, wonderful man." Tom understood from her story that his father had done more than fix her furnace—he had brought her a few moments of joy during a time of utmost loneliness and fear.

The other account came from Pete O'Connell, a man who had worked for many years with "Mickey" Derringer and was there with him when he died. "I've never seen a man so crazy about his kids as your dad was," Pete said to Tom and his sister (Alice stood by Tom's side during most of the reception). "He loved the two of you very much, spoke about you all the time. And he wasn't ashamed to do it. Most men don't say anything at all about their kids, and the ones that do will brag about all their accomplishments, but when the kids slip up a little bit, maybe make a bad decision somewhere along the line, they're quick to tell you everything that's wrong with kids today. But not Mickey, not your dad." Pete said he had never heard their father say anything but good things about his two children, how proud he was of them, how smart they were, how much hope he had that they would go on to college and make something of their lives. "Your dad was always working for you two, for your future. Don't ever forget that. You'll never have a bigger supporter in your lives than your dad. And whatever you do, remember he's still there with you. He's right by your side. Try to make him proud."

Pete spoke quietly, with difficulty, and Tom could see how shaken this plain, simple, hard-working man had been by his father's death. It humbled him and made him wonder about his own ability to perceive what was real, for his perception of his father was so much different. It was not that he saw his father as the *opposite* of what Pete had said—his father had never been mean or violent, had never belittled or degraded either of his children in any way. It was more that he seemed *absent* during most of their lives, or interested in other things when he had any free time. He was a two-pack a day smoker and a hard drinker, of whiskey mostly, and mostly not at home—he went out to a local bar regularly with buddies from work, and only rarely spent time with his wife and children. When he did, he was usually drunk, although to give him his due, he was a happy drunk, and Tom often wondered if his father's smiling disposition had something to do with all the alcohol he consumed. He was a man who, from the point of view of most who knew him, appeared to embrace life with unaffected good humor, and to find—without having to search very hard or perhaps even search at all—reason to smile and to live cheerfully from day to day, but from Tom's perspective, that reason did not seem to include his family, at least not to Tom as a boy growing up. As an adult, reflecting back on the fact that his real mother—his father's first wife—died in a car crash shortly after Alice was born, Tom suspected his father's behavior was a mask of sorts, hiding some inner pain only his father knew anything about. And if this was true, no one could ever have known how much of an effort it had taken for his father to keep the mask from slipping.

There *were* certainties, though. It was certain that Tom had loved his father deeply. It was certain that his father's smoking and drinking—whether intentional or not—had been acts of self-destruction. And it was certain that Tom's mourning, over time, had grown into anger, anger directed first of all at his father—for being absent too much of the time while he was alive, for allowing others to see more clearly than his own family how much his family meant to him, for contributing to his own premature death, his *permanent* absence—and then as the love and loyalty he felt for his father regained sway in his heart, anger of a more generalized kind, anger at the inequity of life, at the essential unfairness of an existence that could allow both his mother and his father to be taken from him by the time he was fifteen. It was certain too that in his thirties when his own son Ben was born, his anger had spurred a rock-solid resolve to do whatever he could to insure he would not follow his father and his grandfather into the grave by virtue of a heart attack. And it was certain that after all the years of discipline and self-denial—the thousands of miles of running, the nearly ascetic severity of his diet, the obsession with cholesterol levels and blood pressure, the daily dose of aspirin for the past fifteen years—the sense of betrayal he was feeling as he drove slowly home through the narrow streets of Portsmouth had circled back again into outrage, outrage at the inescapable conclusion he had come to after absolving his father of all blame and had been trying to circumvent ever since: *it didn't matter whether you thought you had control over your life or not, because life would do with you whatever it wanted.*

"Where have you been?" Fran asked as soon as he walked through the door. She could smell alcohol on his breath when she drew close to him.

"Went to see Dr. Marshall."

"Why?"

"He called earlier and wanted to see me."

"Was that Dr. Marshall on the phone when I was leaving this noon time?"

Tom nodded.

"Why didn't you tell me? I never would have gone to the blood drive if I'd known that."

"That's what I figured."

"They could have done without me."

He did not reply.

"Tom, your health is much more important to me than spending a few hours at the blood drive. I help out there for myself as much as anything. They don't really need *me.*"

He remained silent as he hung up his coat.

"I can't tell you how upset I am that Dr. Mr. Marshall didn't *insist* I be there with you. This is too important for me not to be involved every step of the way." She paused, conscious of the line she was beginning to cross. "What did the doctor have to say?"

Tom turned to face her and she drew even closer to him. "He told me the PSA came back within normal limits but he wants to check it again in about six months. In the meantime, he was concerned about the back pain I've been having so he wrote out a prescription for me." He handed her the slip of paper with the doctor's illegible handwriting on it.

Fran looked over the paper with a stern and skeptical expression. "Why would he have you come in to see him? If he only wanted to tell you everything was okay and give you a prescription, couldn't he have just done that over the phone? Couldn't he have just told you the results and called in the prescription?"

"I suppose he could have," Tom hedged. He had not expected quite such an argumentative response from her. "I guess he must have wanted to allay any fears I might have had. I mean, we *had* been talking about cancer."

Fran peered up at him for a long moment before handing back the paper. She folded her arms on her chest. "So you haven't had this filled yet."

"No."

"What did he say about your back? What does he think is causing the pain?"

"He's assuming it's arthritis, but he'll have a better idea after he sees the x-rays. I had to have some x-rays taken."

"You had x-rays taken tonight?"

He nodded.

"Where?"

"At the hospital."

She looked at him quizzically. "Why do you have alcohol on your breath?"

The question did not come as a surprise to him, although he had no ready answer. "The hospital has a new procedure for dealing with patient anxiety about cancer," he said, deciding to try for humor. He took a step forward and held out his arms to her. Reluctantly she entered the enveloping circle but held back, her hands against his chest, in order to look at him directly. There was nothing about her expression that suggested humor would be welcome. "They administer a shot of your choice if you think you need it. I chose Scotch."

Her eyes narrowed and she strained backward against his hands. "Why would you have had anxiety about cancer after the doctor had just assured you you don't have it?" There was not even the slightest suggestion of levity in her voice. "Are you not telling me something I should know?"

"Look, it's been a very trying day. After I left the hospital I stopped off to have a drink. That's all." He sought to draw her to him and at last she released the tension against his hands and came forward into his embrace. He stroked her hair, inhaled its pleasing fragrance. The light brown that her hair had been for most of their lives together—shoulder length, with a sheen of gold in certain lights—had given way entirely now to silver gray, but it was still silken to the touch and possessed a smell as sweet and distinct to her as ever.

"I just don't find anything funny in the possibility you might have cancer," she said. Her face rested lightly against his chest. Her hands were gentle upon his back.

The words touched him to the core, defining for him exactly the way he felt himself, and a wave of shame and embarrassment washed over him at his feeble attempt to cover his tracks with humor. She deserved better from him than deception and this lame, underlying play for sympathy.

He pressed her tighter to himself and thought of how much he would like to make love to her right now, how much he would like to try to put right what had been going all wrong, but even in the thinking of it he was conscious of the fear and uncertainty that had been undermining everything in his life these days. Whether it was because of this fear or solely because of real physical limitations he did not know, but for the past couple of years he had become less and less of a lover to Fran than he had been in the previous thirty-two years of their marriage. It was a fact that caused him great anguish not only because he expected more of himself as a man—stretching all the way back to high school sexuality had been important to defining who he was, to viewing himself as potent and virile, capable of giving and receiving sensual pleasure with a woman he loved—but more importantly because for him the physical act of lovemaking was a means of *expressing* himself, of *communicating* in a way that reached more profoundly down inside him than words ever could. To be sure, his lovemaking with Fran was often primarily physical, sometimes quick and passionate, sometimes ordinary and mechanistic, arising from and satisfying the libido in each of them, but at its purest and best he believed it was far more than that. The soft press of fingers to fingers and lips to lips, the countless slow and tender caresses, touch leading each to explore every part of the other's body and lingering where it would without hurry or shame, the ultimate conjoining of their bodies—all of it took him outside of himself, obliterated self entirely, and at the same time took him so deeply within himself that he felt his soul becoming one with hers, felt a sense of connection and understanding that he believed was as close to true joy as was possible for two people to experience together in life. There were not words for this. "I love you" was nice to say and hear—reassuring, perhaps even necessary—but it did not begin to approach the depth and intensity of feeling he believed he could express through making love to Fran. And although this belief had certainly not diminished in his heart, his physical capabilities *had* diminished, deserting him so often in recent months and especially in recent weeks that he feared failure nearly as much as he feared the loss of something so fundamental to his being. It had become easier simply to avoid intimacy than to attempt it, but in its absence his heart was aching.

"There's nothing funny about it to me either," he said quietly.

Chapter Five

Preventive Maintenance

Tom was in the garage making sure the snow blower was ready for the predicted snowstorm when the telephone rang. He realized he could probably not get to it quickly enough, and Fran was out shopping for a few last-minute items to take with them to Ben and Marie's for tomorrow's Thanksgiving dinner, so he just let it ring until the machine picked up. He would check the message later.

When he fired up the snow blower the loud echoing reverberations of it and the discharge of carbon monoxide within the garage provoked an involuntary shudder in him and a sensation akin to fear, although it disappeared promptly as he engaged first gear and steered the machine through the open bay door. Even though it was now more than twenty years old the snow blower proved once again to be in good working order, which was no surprise given the meticulous care he took each spring to store it away for the season. His theory was that if you spent a little extra time on preventive maintenance in the spring by doing such things as greasing the gears, changing the spark plug and the oil, painting and waxing where needed, and running a fuel stabilizer through the engine, then in the winter when you really needed the machine it would be ready to go. There was nothing worse than having to fight with such a heavyweight beast as a snow blower in the middle of a blizzard when you had to deal with sub-zero wind chill, pelting snow, and metal colder to the touch than ice. Far better to pamper the beast in the spring and test it now. The dead of winter was too late.

Satisfied that the machine was fit and ready for use, he steered it back into its niche along the rear wall and shut off the engine, musing about the curious physical response he had just experienced. Then he noticed all the other winter equipment arranged neatly along the side wall, alpine skis and cross-country skis and snowshoes suspended from wooden pegs and nails, crates along the floor containing ice skates and winter boots—correlatives of pleasure that appeared as nothing but fixtures for much of the year until the arrival of that very snow and ice which even he, who loved the cold, alternately greeted as the joy and the bane of winter.

The thought of skiing gave him pause. He had finally broken down and had the doctor's prescription filled, in part due to Fran's insistence that living with pain when you didn't have to made absolutely no sense, and the result had been a modest reduction of pain and a modest increase in physical activity. Still, he wondered if he would be able to ski at all this season. *Or ever again.* The thought came to him with a sudden pang of doubt and dismay.

He had been skiing ever since he was six or seven when he received his first pair of skis for Christmas. The skis were nothing more than a toy, really, wooden slats with rawhide sleeves that tied around his galoshes, and the only place for him to ski was the Bandstand Hill, a small knoll only a short walk from his house where other kids would gather after a snowstorm to sled. The skis had no edges and no support, but after his first wobble-legged run straight down the slope (turning was not a consideration because it was not yet even a concept in his mind—*rapid* acceleration, staying upright, and *not falling* were the only things he was conscious of), the speed and the sensation of the wind rushing past and the excitement of feeling himself every instant on the edge of a disastrous fall had him hooked for life. He wanted more of such passion.

And as the years passed he did have more of it. In high school he went on ski trips with friends, trips that made lifelong impressions on him: there was the terror he felt his first time at Cannon Mountain when he slowed to a stop upon the ridge of a trail called "Avalanche" and, peering down, realized two impossible truths—that he could not see much of the trail below because it appeared to drop off the face of the earth at a ninety degree angle, and that as he stood there trembling in disbelief while his more experienced buddies took off ahead of him, there was *no turning back;* there was the exalted feeling of camaraderie and the rapture of independence he had experienced during a weekend trip to Vermont when he and three friends, beyond the overnight purview of adults for the first time in their lives, had found a place to stay for two dollars a night—a quaint flophouse called "Toad Hall" with a choice of bunk beds or mattresses on the floor—had eaten well each day (eggs and bacon for breakfast, pizza for dinner), and had managed to con someone over twenty-one into buying Maneshewicz wine for them each night—all this in addition to the skiing itself, which was the best he had ever experienced up to that point; there was the profound sense of loneliness, of utter isolation despite being with friends upon one memorable trip to Wildcat when brutal winds and arctic cold blew across from the broad white expanse of Mount Washington; and there was the serendipity on another overnight trip to Vermont of waking one morning to ten inches of the lightest snow imaginable, and of the silken quiet of first tracks on the mountain and the absolute bliss, the pure *joie de vivre* of skiing powder for the first time ever, and of falls that were not so much uncontrolled mishaps as welcome slides into the embrace of the snow, and of laughter welling up from nowhere and overflowing into the silence. There had been *many* times while skiing over the years when his exuberance for the speed and the freedom and the almost unbearable beauty of the mountains in winter had been so intense he found himself spontaneously hooting out loud as he flew down a trail.

Skiing had also been a part of his life with Fran for every winter since they first met. It was the main course of weekend getaways in the years immediately following college, with the warmth of a fireplace, lots of sex, and dining out also on the menu as part of *apres ski*. And although it suffered fits and starts as new responsibilities—such as Ben's birth and early childhood—came into their lives, skiing continued through the years. By the time Ben was three he began to join them regularly, and by the time he was a teenager he was off with *his own* friends and developed his own powerful love of the sport.

Tom remembered that once he took a day off from work just to ski with Ben, who was perhaps only five at the time. It was a sunny day in March, warm, with a gentle breeze blowing, the conditions not quite spring skiing but not far off either. They were skiing at a moderate-sized area called Gunstock, and for the better part of the day they skied without a hitch. Ben had taken a single private lesson when he was four, and ever since that time had been an independent skier—no more pitching forward into his parents' waiting arms. Tom marveled at the ease with which Ben was able to get on the T-bars and chairlifts and snowplow his way down terrain Tom himself had not mastered until he was more than twice Ben's age. They ate their bagged lunch outside on a sunny deck, Ben with the rosy cheeks and simple oblivious good humor of a child, Tom with a sense of pride and well-being that he had been hoping to experience on the ski slopes with his son since Ben was born, and that he now realized—the day having arrived—was even more satisfying than he had hoped for.

In the afternoon they tackled more challenging trails than they had skied in the morning. Usually Tom would hover just behind to make sure Ben stayed in control, but occasionally he would ski ahead and turn to watch his son come down the trail, or he would let Ben go first and watch him descend a ways by himself, proud of his son and fearful for him at the same time, his emotions intensifying as the distance between them increased, as Ben—receding down the slope below him and passing farther and farther beyond his influence—seemed to grow smaller and more vulnerable by the second. At the slightest indication of trouble, whether real or imagined, he would bolt down to Ben's side and call out to him, "Hey, buddy, how're you doing?" "Okay," Ben would say without stopping or turning his gaze from the trail ahead, without any awareness of his father's need, and the moment's anguish would pass.

Tom stopped frequently that afternoon so that Ben would not get too tired, and he used the breaks to point out the magnificent views of Lake Winnepesaukee and to identify Mt. Washington and some of the other mountains to the north and west. Toward the end of the day clouds moved in and the temperature dropped, causing the surface of the snow, which had been softened by the sun, to grow harder and quicker. Tom was ready to call it quits but Ben pleaded for another run, so they made their way over to the summit chair one more time. There was no one else in line and the lifthouse clock read 3:58, two minutes before closing time.

"Last run," the lift attendant advised when they they slid onto the boarding area.

After skiing down from the summit cone to a trail junction not far below, Tom suggested they take a trail called "Recoil." He thought they had skied every intermediate trail on the mountain that afternoon, but there it was—a blue square next to a trail they had somehow missed. It made no difference to Ben, so they skied blithely ahead more or less side by side until they came to a section that was steeper than anything they had been on that day. Tom made the mistake of skiing almost to the bottom of the section before realizing the steepness might be a problem for Ben. When he finally stopped and turned to see how Ben was doing, he saw Ben stuck at the crest of the pitch about two hundred feet above him, paralyzed with fear. Ben had dutifully remained in the snowplow wedge, but all forward motion had ceased, his weight was back, and his tiny legs, trembling, looked about to buckle.

"Come on, Ben, you can do it," Tom called up. "Just go back and forth across the trail in nice slow turns. You can do it. I *know* you can."

Ben's legs buckled a bit more and he slid haltingly forward a couple of feet, but then he caught himself and did not move again.

"Come on, Ben."

"I can't," Ben shouted back.

"You *can*, I know you can. All you have to do is make big wide turns and go slow across the trail. Then it gets a lot easier down here where I am."

"I *can't*," Ben cried out again, and Tom could see Ben's head fall to his chest and his shoulders begin to heave.

"Okay, buddy, I'll be right up. Turn your skis sideway to the mountain so you don't fall and I'll be right up there."

"I *can't*," came the anguished reply.

"Okay, hold on. Just hold on, I'm coming." Tom began to skate-ski and sidestep his way back up the slope as quickly as he could, never taking his eyes off his son. The snow was icier now than it had been for most of the day and it was hard to get an edge to hold, but he felt a powerful urgency to continue climbing quickly. He did not know how much longer Ben could keep his legs under him.

"Almost there, buddy, hang on," he said when he drew within twenty feet. As if some inner mechanism informed him it was all right to let go once his father reached a certain point below him, Ben fell back and began to slide down the slope out of control. Tom moved to block his path and reached out with his arms to absorb the impact. Once he had stopped the momentum he wrapped his arms around Ben and held him tight for a moment. He could feel his son's heart pounding and tremors coursing through his small body. Then he drew back and saw that Ben's face was red and tears were streaming from his eyes.

"Why did you leave me?" Ben accused.

"I'm sorry," Tom said. "You've been doing such a great job all day I guess I just didn't realize this would be so tough."

He waited for the sobs to subside a bit before pressing ahead to the issue of how to proceed down the rest of the slope, but Ben beat him to it.

"I don't want to ski anymore," Ben said with bitter certainty.

He held Ben by the shoulders and shook him gently. "Hey, Ben, buddy, come on. Everybody gets a little scared once in a while. It's no big deal. We can get down this trail together."

"I don't want to."

"Well what do you suggest we do?"

"I don't know. Get a helicopter."

The wind had begun to pick up and Tom felt the cold of it as though he were experiencing it through Ben's body instead of his own. He disengaged himself from Ben and said, "Look, let's just try to make one or two turns here and see how it goes, okay? I'll go first, then you follow me and do exactly what I do."

"No! I *can't*. I don't *want* to." Ben sat back on the snow and began to slide downhill before Tom latched onto him again.

"Ok, ok. Let's try something else, Ben, all right? Can you do that for me?"

"What?"

"Here, I'll make a wedge, and you make a wedge inside of mine, and we'll ski down together. Ok?"

Ben was beyond reasoning by this point, so Tom simply bent over to help Ben spread his booted feet and skis within the wedge of his own skis, and thus joined they traversed their slow and precarious way down the steep pitch. "That wasn't so bad, was it?" Tom said, but Ben would not answer.

It took a good deal of time and considerable cajoling to convince Ben that he must ski the rest of the way—at least a mile and a half—on his own, but eventually Ben allowed his skis to slide forward with exaggerated slowness and caution.

"That's it, Ben!" he called out, and in such halting, tentative fashion they wound their way slowly, *very* slowly, down the mountain. Ben had regressed to a level well below where he had started skiing in the morning, but at least he was skiing on his own, and Tom realized with a sharp stab of regret this was about all he could expect from his son right now.

By the time they reached the bottom of the trail light had begun to fade, and Tom noticed they were being shadowed by a ski patrolman. He had been so preoccupied with Ben that he did not realize until that moment how quickly night was coming on, and how quiet it had grown. The ski patrolman was dark and indistinct and the trees on either side of them stood like tall black sentinels lining the white corridor they followed. It occurred to him that he had never been on a mountain so late in the day, never been the last one on the trail, and he shivered to think of how Ben must be feeling right now.

They were quiet and perfunctory in the lodge as they went about the business of getting their boots off (Tom kneeling to help Ben, warming his son's cold toes between his hands) and gathering up their belongings. Red-cheeked and sullen, his dark hair tousled, Ben grudgingly accepted a cup of hot chocolate and sipped it while Tom ran a load of their gear out to the car. They both carried their skis back—it was Tom's hard and fast rule: if you wanted to ski, no matter your age, you carried your own skis. No exceptions. Not even after such a long and demoralizing last run.

A few minutes into the ride home, though, he sought rapprochement. "Good day today, wasn't it, Benj?"

Ben gave a silent, half-hearted nod without looking over. He was sitting at the far end of the front seat, his back straight upright and slightly rigid, his legs, in thick snow pants, stretched straight out before him with his small booted feet barely extending beyond the front edge of the seat. His head did not reach up high enough for him to see above the dashboard. It occurred to Tom that the front seat of a car, like so much in life, was not meant to accommodate a child.

"Sorry about that last run, buddy. I didn't know."

Ben offered no response at all this time, merely sat motionless and without expression. After two or three more such attempts met with only a shrug or a one-word answer, Tom gave up and drove on in silence, pondering what seemed to him a cruel truth, that often in life those very things which provided the greatest joy could also provide the greatest sorrow. His heart ached at the thought, though when he looked over and saw his son curled fast into sleep, mouth slightly open and body now limp and relaxed, he realized it could not be any other way.

That day like so many others spent on the ski slopes, with its epiphanies and disappointments, had been etched deeply into his memory, and as he stood there in the garage contemplating the ski equipment and what it signified to him he wondered again whether he would use it any time soon. He had been hoping to ski this season with his grandson. Teddy was about the same age as Ben when he and Fran had first strapped skis on Ben's feet, steered him down the smallest of hills, and hoped for the best. Ben was barely past walking, really. Still in the toddler stage. And here now—impossible as it was to believe—it was his *grandson's* turn, and he did not know if he would be a part of it.

The best laid plans of mice and men, he thought, and remembered suddenly another of his long-lost hopes, something he had been yearning to do for many years now: to ski out west with Ben, just the two of them.

He had only skied out west once in his life, back during winter break one year when he was in college and a friend named Brian Finneran, who had bounced around the west for a while after high school and done a lot of skiing, convinced him that for the money (which was of course a paramount concern in those days) they couldn't possibly do better than to ski in Utah, specifically at Alta. So the two of them scraped together enough money to get themselves out there in Brian's rusty old Chevy pickup, which had a cap on the back that provided them with enough shelter—along with a small kerosene heater, some rolls and a couple of sleeping bags—to sleep right in the back of the truck in the parking lot of the ski area. The skiing was beyond anything Tom had ever imagined despite Brian's frequent testimonials that he wasn't going to believe how good it was.

Once they got out of Salt Lake City and up into Little Cottonwood Canyon it seemed as though there was snow *everywhere,* and it was not at all the sort of snow he was used to growing up in New England—the sort of heavy, wet snow that was good for snowballs and building forts along the roadside—

this snow seemed lighter than down feathers, deeper *by far* than anything he had ever experienced, and *without ice.* Ice did not appear to exist in this realm of airy whiteness. It snowed a couple of times while they were there and when it did, visibility was nonexistent—the conditions were truly whiteout conditions—and the snow accumulated so rapidly that he found himself skiing in untracked powder on every run. Of course, between the falling snow and the snow sprayed up into his face as he skied he couldn't *see* what he was skiing in anyway, and there was a peculiar sensation of vertigo that occasionally had him not knowing which direction was up or down, left or right, whether he was turning with the fall line or against it, and the result was that he sometimes felt completely unbalanced and disoriented, but none of that mattered against the incessant feeling of floating, not of scraping along atop a steep narrow trail and fighting the mountain and the ice with sharpened edges and perpetual wariness as he had done nearly all of his skiing life but of floating, of moving smoothly and softly and quietly *through* the snow, through bowls and chutes and vast treeless expanses of whiteness, nothing but whiteness, the only danger that of being lulled by the sheer pleasure of it all into floating right off a cliff or setting off an avalanche on one of the countless steep pitches. On the days when it was not snowing— and they had a few of those as well—the deep azure blue sky was like what he had experienced in New England only in October, on the very best of days, perfect days, and yet here it seemed as though if it was not snowing so hard you couldn't see anything, thereby creating perfect snow for skiing, it was perfectly blue and cloudless, with the temperature somewhere around twenty-five degrees and plenty of deep powder wherever you wanted to go.

It was into this spectacular winter world that he had always dreamed of taking Ben, *passionately* dreamed it—just the two of them—but it had never happened, and now it appeared that it never would. At first he had wanted to wait until Ben became a more accomplished skier so that he could handle the challenging terrain they would ski together, but as Ben grew into his teenage years and did become a better skier, he skied with his friends and wanted no part of skiing with just Dad. By the time Ben had finished with college he was seeing Marie, married her not long after that, and the prospect of father and son traipsing out west to spend some time together skiing seemed like nothing but a lark, a precious fantasy, and—until this moment—slipped away from consciousness like so many other dreams exposed to wakeful daylight.

He returned to the kitchen with a heavy heart and saw the blinking red message light on the telephone's answering machine. He pressed the button and listened: "Mr. Derringer, this is Doctor Marshall's office calling. The doctor happened to notice that he hadn't received your x-rays yet from the hospital, and the hospital has no record of them being taken. He wanted you to know it's important that he see them as soon as possible, and if you have any questions or concerns, to please give us a call. The number here is..." *Give him credit,* Tom thought as he deleted the message, *there aren't many doctors nowadays who would follow up like that.*

Chapter Six

Thanksgiving

"Thank you so much!" Marie said after greeting Fran and Tom at the door with hugs and receiving from Fran a bottle of white wine, a wedge of brie, and a bag of flavored coffee beans.

"Well, I happened to be over at Tuttle's yesterday and I just know how much you and Ben enjoy wine and cheese, so I thought I'd bring some over today. They have such a wonderful selection there. The coffee isn't ground, though. I hope you don't mind."

"No, that's great. We prefer it that way. Thanks!"

"And here's the promised pumpkin pie," Tom said, holding out a foil-covered glass pie plate, "which was made in no small part with the help of my tender loving words of encouragement."

Teddy came running in from the kitchen shouting, "Grammy! Grampa! You're here!" and leaped into Fran's arms first and then reached over for a hug from his grandfather as well.

"Happy Thanksgiving, Mom, Dad," Ben said, following Teddy in from the kitchen. He gave his mother a hug and a kiss on the cheek. "It's good to have you here." He shook his father's hand. "How've you been, old man? How's the back?"

"Better, thanks. It hasn't been bothering me quite as much lately."

"Tell them the whole story, Tom," Fran said. She was still holding Teddy in her arms. "Your father finally broke down and went to see Dr. Marshall a while ago, and the doctor gave him a prescription for a pain reliever that seems to have been working—so far, at least. Knock on wood." She searched around for a moment and then rapped her knuckles lightly on a desk nearby.

"Mom, that's probably just pressboard, not real wood," Ben laughed, "but I guess it'll work."

"That's great news," Marie said. "What did the doctor think was causing the pain?"

There was an awkward silence for a moment over who should answer the question, but Marie's gaze finally settled upon Tom and he said, "Just what I had figured, arthritis."

"I guess you were a pretty good judge."

"So it seems."

"You must know your body, then. I often think if we would only listen more to what our bodies are telling us, we could prevent a lot of the bad things that happen to us, or at least catch sickness and disease before they get too serious. The problem is that most of the time we don't listen very well."

Tom nodded. "I think you're right."

"Did you have x-rays taken?" Ben asked.

"That's the protocol."

"And?"

"It appears I have the most common form of arthritis. It's called degenerative joint disease—in my case, of the spine. Most people will develop some form of it if they live long enough, so I guess I can't really complain."

"It's a lot better than what the doctor first feared," Fran added. "Initially he was afraid it might be prostate cancer, so we were both relieved to find out it wasn't that. Arthritis can be very debilitating, and I don't want to downplay the pain Tom has been experiencing, but at least it's not cancer. I thank God for that."

"What made him suspect prostate cancer in the first place?" Ben asked. Again there was a moment of confusion over who should answer, but Ben's unequivocal gaze made it clear the question was intended for his father.

"When you get to be my age doctors routinely check the prostate during an exam. In my case, Dr. Marshall thought the prostate was somewhat enlarged, so he ran tests to make sure it wasn't cancerous. I guess it's a pretty standard thing to be concerned about in men by the time they're fifty."

"So are you all set or do you need to go back for another checkup?"

"I don't need to go back."

"Tom," Fran said with a note of alarm in her voice, "I thought the doctor wanted to see you again in six months?"

"Well, yes," Tom said, backtracking, "he did say that, but I thought Ben was talking about right now. In any case, enough about my ailments. I don't want to talk about them any more. We're here for a celebration, so let's celebrate. How about a glass of that wine? I'd like to make a toast if anyone would like to join me."

"I'll join you, Grampa!" Teddy blurted out, prompting laughter from all.

"That's my boy."

Marie gathered glasses for everyone and juice for Teddy while Ben opened the bottle of wine and did the pouring.

"Yesterday I had the snow blower out just to be sure it would be ready for this storm they're predicting—which, by the way, I haven't heard anything about today. Has anyone heard a recent forecast?"

"It's supposed to start early this evening," Ben said, "with maybe several inches of snow accumulating quickly at first and then changing over to sleet or freezing rain later on. A nasty mess, as usual."

"It's awfully early in the season for this," Fran said. "I hope it's not a sign of what the rest of the winter will be like."

"In any case, yesterday while I was working on the snow blower I was thinking a lot about skiing, and about getting you started this year, young boy," Tom said to his grandson. He smiled and pointed at Teddy, but out of regard for the juice refrained from his fond custom of poking his grandson in the midsection. Teddy smiled in return and shrank back a little in anticipation of the poke but managed not to spill his juice. "So, my toast is two toasts, really: first, let's give thanks for the prosperity that brings us all together for this wonderful meal we'll be having shortly." He raised his glass and said, "To all that we have to be thankful for..." clinked it gently against the others, and led everyone in taking a sip. "Second, let's toast the future. To continued health and prosperity—may tonight's snow be the start of a joyful winter that gives us all a chance to ski together sometime!" He led them once more in clinking and sipping from their glasses, but this time he felt beneath the warmth of his wishes the chill breath of his own deceptions.

The snow began to fall lightly at first and had about it that quality of quiet and simplicity that suggested an idyllic winter scene by Normal Rockwell or Currier and Ives. Teddy looked out the window and bounced up and down on one of the couches in excitement, Marie called the snow "pretty," and the adults in general agreed that if it amounted to no more than an inch or two, they would all welcome it. It was not long though before the wind began to pick up and the snow started coming down harder, accumulating at a rate that Tom knew would be far from idyllic to have to contend with later on, especially if it turned to sleet or freezing rain as Ben had suggested. He put off leaving for as long as he could while the snow continued to accumulate, but reluctantly they were all forced to agree on the need to cut short the festivities so that he and Fran could get home before the traveling got *too* bad.

After they had arrived home he gazed out the window and wondered what to do as the storm continued to intensify. He could hear the cracks and groans of the house under the assault of the wind, and he could see in the glow of the outside lights that the snow appeared as if it were being driven horizontally. There was a fury out there that he had never seen in the month of November. On the one hand he hated the thought of going out in the cold and darkness before the storm had finished—it was so much easier to deal with in the light of day, even in the near whiteout conditions that sometimes developed and made visibility as impossible during the day as during the night. And after a full and satisfying Thanksgiving dinner in the company of his family and the comfortable torpor that was already beginning to settle in here at home, it seemed the most unlikely thing in the world to have to go back out and do battle with cold, wind, and snow. On the other hand the thought of waiting until a foot or more had fallen and then having that capped off with the weight of sleet and freezing rain possessed all the appeal of shoveling wet cement, which was pretty close to what the consistency of the snow would be if he waited too long.

"I'm going out," he said at last to Fran, who had just finished putting away the casserole dishes she had brought to the dinner and was about to settle down to do some knitting in the living room.

"Don't you think you should wait? It's still snowing pretty hard."

"Yes, it is, but if I wait too long I don't know if I'll be able to move it. You heard what Ben said about it turning to rain."

"Then let's pay someone to plow us out. It's not like we can't afford it."

"There's also Mrs. Goodwin to think about."

"She'll be fine. She won't need to be going anywhere in *this* weather."

"I understand that, but what if someone needs to get *to* her? What if we were to lose power—which you know happens all too often around here—and an emergency vehicle needed to get to her? I don't want to see her cut off."

"You're a good man, Tom, sweet and generous, but I still don't think you need to go out now, especially not with the way your back has been. If you're concerned about Mrs. Goodwin, which I am too, then let's just call her and make sure she's okay. She can always come and stay with us."

But he *did* need to go out, and for reasons he could not thoroughly explain to her. He had been self-reliant for most of his life—for *all* of his adult life—and he had been helping Mrs. Goodwin, their only close neighbor, for as long as he could remember, for as long as her husband had been dead, which had to be at least twenty years now, and he was not about to stop if he could help it. Then too, he felt a certain amount of atonement was in order for things he could not yet confess to her, things that were as yet a kind of fiction, if not outright lies, and in a deep and primitive part of his soul he sought purification through hard work, as though hard work were the alchemy that would transmute fiction into reality and absolve him from the sins he was beginning to commit with more and more regularity. He had begun to feel a rift growing between them, a rift caused by him and separating them more and more each day, as if he had set himself on an ice floe that was drifting away from the mainland where she lived, and the only way back to her, the only way to close the rift, was through perseverance and hard work and force of will. If he would only dedicate himself with enough persistence and singularity of purpose, there would be no pain and no falsity and no separation.

"That's a good idea. Why don't you give her a call. But I still have to get out there before the changeover."

Once again when he set off the reverberating roar of the snow blower in the garage he felt that peculiar shudder of something like fear, although when he opened one of the bay doors and confronted the furious force of the wind, he found himself bolstered by the sound, bucked up by the machine's power and glad for its ability to meet force with force. This was no ordinary storm. The snow was wind driven and heavy and accumulating fast, which pleased him in an odd way because it justified his decision to get out and deal with it now rather than wait until tomorrow. The wind came from the northeast in stinging cold gusts that whipped slivers of snow and ice into his face despite the hood he had drawn around his head like an anorak.

He cut a two-foot swath the length of his driveway and on through the thick bank that plows had already pushed up at the end, then continued along the road until he reached Mrs. Goodwin's driveway. She had turned on an outside light for him, as was her custom, and was now standing behind the fogged up glass storm door watching him work, a small shadowy figure against the lighted room behind her, old and frail, looking on and waving to him. He waved back and then with both hands made a pushing motion for her to go inside, but she remained by the door. When he was satisfied with his work he turned and waved to her again and motioned for her to go inside, but again she remained by the door until he had made his way to the end of her driveway.

It was very dark along the stretch of road between her driveway and his, darker still because there was no light from the lamppost at the end of his driveway. The bulb must have burned out while he was over at Mrs. Goodwin's. He could see well enough down the haloed length of his driveway to recognize that the swath he'd cut earlier had already been filled in with another inch or two of snow; here at the end all was shadowy darkness except for the dim white of newly fallen snow.

He continued working slowly and methodically, driving the old machine again and again into the weighty mass of plowed snow and hearing it strain with the effort, until at last he realized there was no snow coming out of the chute. *Must be plugged,* he thought, disengaging the clutch so that he could check the chute.

Sure enough, a thick plug of compressed snow had jammed itself into the chute, requiring him to dislodge it manually. He had no tools with him so he was forced to pry it out using his already soaked and freezing gloved fingers. As he dug at the unyielding wedge in a kind of mounting anger, he heard the engine begin to accelerate on its own and sound a high frenzied pitch that he had never heard from it before. He watched in dumbfounded amazement as it continued to accelerate and then to shake and smoke. Instinctively he jammed the throttle into the "off" position to shut the machine down, but nothing happened. The machine continued to whine and shake and smoke as if it possessed a life of its own and were undergoing the mechanical equivalent of an epileptic seizure. At last the machine chugged and coughed a couple of times and then went still. Dark smoke continued to come from it in wisps that the wind carried off immediately, and he could hear the hiss and sizzle of snow pelting against the superheated metal of the exhaust, but otherwise the machine was still and silent. Lifeless. *Dead.* He realized it was not just an idle thought but a certainty. *Dead.* Yet he could not accept it and could not believe it, had still to prove it. He put the throttle back into the "start" position, made sure the clutch was in neutral, pulled the starter cord. The only sound was an undifferentiated whirring like the noise made by a vacuum. Not even the faintest suggestion the engine would fire and come back to life. He tried adjusting the choke although he knew this too would be futile. Pulled on the cord again. Again nothing but the whirring vacuum sound. *Useless piece of shit!* he shouted inwardly and then out loud as he pulled again and again until on one pull a sharp stabbing pain shot through his low back and dropped him to his knees as abruptly as if he had been knifed from behind. He closed his eyes and remained motionless on his knees for a moment. In that moment there was no pain and no snow and no storm, merely darkness and the sounds of his own quick shallow breathing and the beating of his heart. It occurred to him with a kind of detached calmness and an absurdly sensible logic that if he could only stay right here he would be all right, but he knew that he must move and that it was movement, above all, that he feared. He had begun to fear it some time ago but had not known until this moment how much he feared it. And this too was absurd because he loved to move: loved to run—in high school he had been the fastest sprinter on the track team; loved to ski, whether in short quick turns on very steep slopes or in long, arcing parabolas at high speed; loved to skate—had once skated miles along a frozen river with Fran when they were college sweethearts; loved to backpack and to climb mountains; loved to wade rivers and to cast a fly rod; loved simply to walk—whether strolling along the beach in the summer or snowshoeing in the deep quiet powder of the woods in winter. And here he was now on his knees, immobile and scared, taking in shallow, careful breaths because he feared the excess movement of a deep breath, he who had not believed in God since he was a child offering undirected entreaties that he not be made to feel such pain again. *Please, please, not again. Not like that again. Please.* And yet he must move, he must. *Must. Move.*

But in the movement was the pain, and more pain beyond that, and in the pain the falling, and in the falling the recognition that the pain was receding into darkness.

Fran had watched him head down the length of their driveway and turn toward Mrs. Goodwin's, then had ceased paying attention for a time except to be aware in a peripheral way of the distant muffled sound of an engine at work. Like the sound of a lawnmower off in the distance in the summertime, there was something reassuring about the low, barely audible drone of the snow blower doing its valuable brute work. She only wished that it were not Tom operating it.

She had decided that she would start knitting this very night, and with Tom out working it gave her a perfect opportunity to do so. Earlier she and Marie had been cleaning up together in the kitchen after dinner when Marie had said to her in quiet confidence, "I've got good news, Fran. Teddy's going to be having a brother or a sister in June."

"That's wonderful, Marie! When did you find out?"

"Just yesterday. Ben knows, of course, but he's the only other person I've told. We didn't want to make too much of it tonight because of Teddy—it seems a bit early to be telling him about it."

"Of course, I agree. Is it all right if I tell Tom later? He'll be thrilled!"

"Absolutely. We just didn't want to say anything to both of you publicly tonight—you know, have a toast or something—because of Teddy. Ben hoped he'd have a chance to talk to his dad tonight, but I'm not sure that's going to happen. It's impossible to pry Teddy away from his grandfather. He's just so crazy about Tom!"

"I think the prying would have to go both ways. I'll talk to him about it later tonight though if Ben doesn't have a chance.

Oh, it's just such wonderful news, Marie! I'm so happy for you—for all of us!"

But it had already been snowing heavily for quite a while by the time they left Ben and Marie's, and she decided it would be better—less distracting to her absentminded and all-too-distractible husband—to wait and talk about it after they were safely back home. Then as soon as they were home Tom couldn't rest until he'd gone out to put his notions of order on the storm's chaos, and it made no sense to her to broach the subject until after he'd come back inside when he could relax. He was a funny man that way, often trying to control what in her view couldn't be controlled, to create order where none was apparent. He had always had a hard time accepting notions of randomness or uncertainty, and she had wondered more than once over the years whether that was the result of his training as an architect or the reason he had become an architect in the first place. *To find perfection in an imperfect world.* Laudable, perhaps. Or foolish. She was never quite sure which, and often found herself vacillating from one instance of it to the next. But it was a character trait that she had come to love in him, this unwillingness to accept the imperfect without question, without a struggle for something better.

And the world certainly was imperfect. The thought of Marie's pregnancy brought that back all too clearly when she remembered the mixed emotions of her own pregnancy with Ben. For many of the months she carried him she felt morning sickness *all day,* the nausea so intense at times that she could hardly move, thought it would be easier and perhaps better for her to die rather than to suffer such torture one more week, one more day, one more *hour.* The morning sickness grew so severe at one point that she was not gaining weight and showed such dangerously lowered fluid levels that she had to be admitted to the hospital to receive fluids intravenously. People told her to try to bear up, even to cheer up, because it wouldn't last forever, it was only temporary, shouldn't continue beyond the first few months *(months!—did they have any idea what that meant to her?)*, but they were wrong in this just as they were wrong in the notion that she would ultimately feel great joy in her pregnancy. There were isolated moments of happiness—when she told Tom initially, when she first heard the heartbeat in the doctor's office, whenever she experienced periods, however brief and fleeting, of the absence of nausea—but these *were* the rare exceptions. The morning sickness did become less acute over time, but right up until the very end it never left entirely, and if she had had to define the prevailing mood of those nine months—honestly and without all the layers of romance with which people preferred to cover up the naked realities of pregnancy—it would have been *grit-your-teeth endurance,* accompanied by the hushed refrain of *Please, God, take this pain from me, let my time pass quickly, let me survive!*

Tom had an especially hard time with her pain and discomfort, felt responsible and wanted constantly to do something about it, would lay his hands upon her belly in futile attempts to draw the misery away from her somehow, pledged to her that if he could take it away and bear the burden of it himself, he would do so in a heartbeat. She believed him and knew that he was sincere, no husband could have been more solicitous of her than he was, and yet there came a point where his anguish for her was almost too great, made her feel worse because in addition to her own pain she must bear his pain as well, and so she learned to cover up what she was feeling, pretend that it wasn't so bad, because the alternative was to carry more than she believed she could bear.

And then came the nightmare of labor and delivery. The blood-tinged fluid when her bag of waters broke followed soon after by excruciating pain at every contraction, Tom huddled near and trying to help in abject futility, and then driving her at breakneck speed to the hospital and there amidst all the bleeding and pain and terror the discovery of the abruption of her placenta, and the clipped whispered concerns about blood loss and low heart rate and fetal distress and then the decision to do a cesarean and the ushering of Tom out of the room (she saw him, white-faced, leaving the room but in the intensity of her self-absorption and worry for her unborn child could afford him no more than a momentary pang of concern) and her learning only after everything had been done the details about how close she had been to losing her child and how she had developed a rare disorder the doctor called "D-I-C" that required a blood transfusion and a hysterectomy to save *her* life. And so she would have no more children.

No, the world, life, was not neat and orderly, and not even close to perfect. It had nearly killed her *and* her baby, but it had given her a healthy son and she had lived to hold him in her arms and to help him grow and to share in the countless joys of his twenty-six years of life, including the birth of his first child and now, God willing, the birth of his second child as well. She could not complain, and she had no right to ask for anything more. Her bond with Ben had been, if anything, closer and more profound throughout his life than if her pregnancy had been smooth and his birth had happened without complication, and if she had sometimes regretted not being able to provide him with a brother or a sister, she had also acknowledged at times, in moments of the starkest honesty in the most private recesses of her heart, that if other children had been a part of her life, she might never have developed the degree of intimacy with Ben that she had. And she would not have wanted to trade that for anything, could not imagine having had anything less than the kind of intuitive connection to each other that they had always had.

She *knew* when Ben was sick or when something was bothering him even before he did. Friends and relatives often commented on how "good" he was when he was a baby, how rarely he cried, how often he smiled, how *lucky* she was to have such a baby, and it pleased her to hear these things not just because it was a compliment, as they intended, to his sanguine nature, but because it meant she understood implicitly (although she never would have suggested it to them) what his needs were. She anticipated when he was hungry and put him to breast before he needed to let her know, and she understood the rhythms of his body so well that she would change him as soon as he needed to be changed, so that he never sat for long in his own messes and his skin was rarely corrupted by burning rashes. It was as if she were privy to his thoughts, or as if in the spilling of blood when he was born there had been some sort of symbiotic understanding created, like that between identical twins, except that their relationship was not of equals but of mother and son. On those rare occasions when he *was* troubled, she would sing to him softly, in the softest and calmest and most languorous voice she could find, rocking him slowly all the while, and he would settle as though under hypnosis. *Your mama does love you,* she would whisper-sing, *like puddin' and pancakes, your mama does love you, yeah, yeah, yeaaah, yeah, yeah.* And she would sing it again and again, long past the time when he would fall asleep, and she would sing, *There's a web like a spider web, made of silver light and shining, spun by the moon, in my room at night. It's a web made to catch a dream, hold it tight 'til I awaken, as if to tell me, dreamin's all right.* And she would sing this too several times, knowing each time she sang it while he slept that it was not for him any longer but for herself that she sang, out of the quiet simple joy of acknowledging the good fortune in her life that couldn't possibly be true even though it was, *as if to tell me, dreamin's all right.*

In the early weeks after Ben was born she felt none of the "blues," the post-partum depression, that the baby books warned about, but she wondered occasionally if Tom harbored any hard feelings toward Ben because of all the difficulties she had experienced during her pregnancy and her horrific labor and delivery and her prolonged recovery afterwards and the ramifications on their plans for at least two children. For a time Tom seemed distant from his newborn son, and she feared the possibility that he blamed his son for everything that had gone wrong. But early one Sunday morning when Ben could not have been more than a month old, she caught him standing before the crib in their room with his back to her. Sunlight was just beginning to peek above the window ledge and fall upon their sleeping infant son. She came up behind him and put her arms around him and rested her head upon his back, and he said to her in a voice trembling with emotion, "I don't know what I would do if anything were ever to happen to him." She could hear that he was having a hard time getting the words past his throat. "I mean, I like to believe he's already had a wonderful life in the short time he's been with us, but I think sometimes about what it would be like if anything ever happened...you know, like that sudden infant...and I don't know what I would do. I don't know if I could handle it." She knew then that all her fears were groundless, and that everything would be all right. "I know what you mean," she said. "I feel the same way. But he *is* a happy baby, and he *has* had a wonderful life so far, and that's all we can possibly give to him." Neither one said anything further, but she felt, she knew, she would never have to worry about Tom again. Ben's presence in their lives was a gift, a blessing, one that she understood from then on meant as much to Tom as to her.

Which was not to say they didn't have their moments over the years when things were rocky—Tom had very high expectations for his son, and the tone of his words to Ben often seemed to her overly harsh and critical. Sometimes, if she felt he was going too far, she would defend Ben, and this might cause a rift between them for a while, but the rift was nearly always short-lived because underneath it all (she was fervently convinced this was the reason) there was love—all the way around. As he grew older, Ben became more and more capable of defending himself, and the two of them, father and son, developed a kind of hard-edged irony, if not ridicule, as their primary tone for communicating with each other. Ben became so adept at the use of sarcasm that more often than not she found herself stepping in to defend *Tom* rather than Ben; but although to this very day the two of them still occasionally took their badinage to a dangerous level, she had never lost faith in the truth of what she saw in Tom that Sunday morning long ago, and as for Ben, she believed she knew the deep channels of his heart better than he knew them himself, at least insofar as his father was concerned, and his father dwelled there just as surely and as irrevocably and as passionately as she did herself. He simply could not speak to his father in the ways he could speak to her, and it was a shame he had not had the opportunity this night to deliver his wonderful news to his father himself. Happy as she was to do it, it would have been far better for Ben to be the bearer of such joyful tidings.

She put the knitting needles down thoughtfully in her lap for a moment, wishing that Ben were here right now to speak to his father when he came in, and in that moment she realized that she no longer heard the drone of the snow blower. It struck her as odd because she had not heard it approach the house, and although she had been lost in thought, she normally never traveled so far away that she was unaware of what was going on nearby. Which was a character trait in her—and one of those differences between her and Tom—that she had often teased him about through the years. What she labeled as his being "unaware" (or, secretly, "oblivious"), he described as his "ability to focus." He could be reading a book or having a conversation and not realize a disagreement was happening right next to him, while she could be listening intently to someone she was speaking with, not missing a word of what the person was saying and not in the least being rude, while being aware of an undercurrent going on between two people in another room. More than once after a party they had both attended they would be driving home together reflecting on the night and comparing impressions, and she would say something like, "Do you think Martha is gay?", and he would have no idea what she was talking about. "Didn't you see..." she would say, and go on to explain in detail the observations behind her question, and he would insist that it didn't seem possible, and they would discover a day or a week or a month later that Martha was leaving her husband of twenty years and pursuing a relationship with a woman they both knew.

She got up from her chair and went over to the window to look out. Snow was still coming down very hard, gusting and swirling in the wind, which made it difficult to see down the length of the driveway. The lights over the garage were on but she realized that the lamppost light at the end of the driveway was not, which struck her as odd because Tom would surely have put that on before heading out. She tried flicking the light switch but nothing happened. The end of the driveway remained dark and obscure. *The bulb must have burned out,* she thought, and then, *he must still be at Mrs. Goodwin's.* She moved to a window that faced Mrs. Goodwin's house but it was dark in that direction as well so she opened the doorway to the front porch and stepped outside, avoiding the several inches of snow that had accumulated on the porch steps and well onto the porch itself. She could hear the wind rushing through the arched and swaying trees and gathering itself into a roar and then relenting a little and then gathering itself into a roar again, and beneath that a sound like that of the ocean, of waves crashing against rocks and shore, and there was something hypnotic and almost supernaturally rhythmic in the swaying trees and the clouds and mists of snow that danced and swirled in the halo of the garage lights. A tremor of fear shivered through her and she told herself to remain calm, not to panic, there must be a good reason for no longer hearing the machine or seeing the plumes of snow it shot into the air. Maybe he was out on the road coming back from Mrs. Goodwin's, out between her driveway and theirs. He wouldn't be blowing snow out there and with the banks as high as they were she probably wouldn't be able to hear him either. Maybe the machine had simply run out of gas and he would be coming into view any moment now cursing his bad luck. Or maybe he had broken one of those—what did he call them, those things he said always broke at the worst possible times, in the coldest possible weather? *Sheer pins.* That was it. Maybe he had broken a sheer pin. She waited a few more moments, but the snow merely continued to fall and the wind continued to lash the trees, and she felt herself growing cold.

Inside, she debated for a moment whether it was foolish of her not to wait longer before going out to look for him. She would have a hard time explaining to him why she was outside all bundled up without having to confess that she was worried about him. At best he would find that generous but amusing, and at worst he might find in it a lack of confidence that amounted to a kind of betrayal. She could almost hear him saying, "I might be getting old, but I'm not *that* old." But she could also hear her own angry retort: *I don't care if you think I'm being foolish. There are all kinds of possibilities that make it* not *foolish. If you were worried about* me, *you know you'd do exactly the same thing,"* and she decided it didn't matter at all how he viewed it. She would do what she must for her own peace of mind.

When she approached the end of the driveway following the swath he had cleared earlier she could make out the low dark hulk of the snow blower but she could not see Tom. Her heart skipped a beat and she raced forward angling herself against the wind and the pelting snow. Then she saw him. He was on his hands and knees in the snow, obscured by the machine. At first she thought he was searching for something there beneath him, or perhaps working on a problem with the machine. But then she realized that he was fumbling about awkwardly and having a difficult time moving, his hands groping as if for a way to push or pull himself upright and finding nothing that could help him.

"Tom!" she called out. He raised his head in response but then lowered it immediately, and she rushed forward to kneel by his side. His hands and knees were buried in the snow already on the ground and his back was getting covered by the falling snow. "Oh, Tom, honey, what's wrong?"

He lifted his head in an effort to look at her but wincing with pain he could not sustain it. "My back," he said as if speaking to the snow directly below him rather than to her. She could barely hear, and bent down next to him. "Something's wrong."

"Can you stand? Can you get up at all? Come on, I'll help you."

"I don't know if I can," he managed. There was a note of uncertainty and fear in his voice that she had never heard before.

"Can you try? Do you want to try? Or do you want to stay here? I can call an ambulance."

He shook his head. "I'll try."

She bent lower, placed her gloved hands next to one of his. "Give me your hand. We'll go slowly, very, very slowly."

He raised a hand to hers and she began to guide him up with excruciating slowness to one knee. His back remained bent and his eyes were closed but he could feel his face contorting and the wind and snow lashing against it though these were distant sensations, as distant as the sounds he knew escaped from him in his effort to maintain control, and that was the only thing that mattered, maintaining control. Above all he did not want to lose control and sink into the darkness again, and so he gave in to her slow helping hands and fought the impulse to rebel against the pain and move faster.

She at once guided him and allowed him to set the pace by which he could raise himself to one knee and then up to his feet, his back bent forward all the while. She had never in all the years they had known each other seen him like this before, not even on that night not so long ago when she had held him in her arms and pledged to him that she would suffer with him through whatever lay ahead but would not allow him to go on as he was without seeking help. She had sensed then but had not yet known that what troubled him was more than a mere bad back. Now she knew, and the knowledge resonated so certainly within her that she trembled with it.

"You're cold," he said. "You shouldn't be out here. I'm sorry."

"I'm all right, darling. It's you who shouldn't be out here. We need to get you inside. Can you make it?"

He was bent forward at a forty-five degree angle, one hand in hers and one hand on her shoulder. He nodded. "I'm okay now," he said, although they both knew it was a lie, and as if to underscore the fact he felt a spasm of pain that doubled him over even further and might have pitched him face first into the snow but for her support. "I can make it," he said. "Just don't let me go."

She was surprised and dismayed by the absence of irony in his words. "I won't let you go," she said, and helped him make his way slowly back inside to the warmth and sanctuary of their home.

Inside, she helped him to take off the outer layers of his clothing and to lie back on the couch near the fireplace. He was trembling from the pain so she went quickly to find the medication Dr. Marshall had prescribed for him.

"When did you take this last?" she said, looking over the label for instructions.

"I don't know, but double what it says." His eyes were closed and she could see that he was trying to control his breathing by inhaling through his nose and exhaling slowly through his mouth.

She did as he said and helped him to take the pills with a glass of water, then helped him to lie back down.

"Thank you," he said, closing his eyes again. "But a shot of Scotch would have been better."

"I'm going to call an ambulance, Tom."

He opened his eyes and took a deep breath. "Don't. Please. I'll be all right. Just let the medication have a chance to kick in."

She found his eyes and saw there the glimmer of something he did not want her to see. "What is it, Tom? What are you afraid of? What are you keeping from me?"

He closed his eyes again and she could see that he was gritting his teeth against a wave of pain. Then the muscles in his jaw relaxed and he said in a controlled and measured voice, "I never went for x-rays."

It took a moment for this to register with her. "So Dr. Marshall has never seen any x-rays of your back?"

He nodded.

"And therefore he doesn't really know that it's arthritis. He doesn't *know* what's wrong." She could feel herself growing angry despite the fact that Tom was still in obvious pain and struggling just to speak.

He kept his eyes closed and shook his head. "He suspects."

"What? What does he suspect?" She could feel her anger intensifying and commingling now with fear.

"Cancer."

"Why? You told me the PSA came back normal."

He shook his head and gritted his teeth again. She could not tell this time whether it was out of physical pain or remorse for the deceptions he had used to mislead her.

"It wasn't normal?"

"It was very high. He wanted me to have a biopsy done."

"And of course that hasn't been done either."

He shook his head slowly but kept his eyes closed and said nothing more.

She felt stunned and didn't know how to respond. It was as if he had just told her he never really loved her, or that he had been having an affair with another woman, the one he truly loved. Anger and outrage mounted inside her alongside disappointment and a profound sense of betrayal. And yet...she had suspected it all along. Not the details, of course. But she had suspected—*known! truthfully*—that something serious was wrong with him, and now she knew also that she would not admit it to herself before. Perhaps *could* not. And was this essentially different from what he had done? Hadn't she kept from him, *from herself,* what she had been afraid to acknowledge, to consider openly? What did it matter that he had possession of more facts, more information from the doctor? There were different ways to know things, and the truth was that she had known as well as if she had had more information, perhaps had known even better, and she had chosen to disregard what she knew and to avoid speaking directly to him about it, had been willing to accept at face value, without questioning, what he told her about his PSA level even though it didn't ring true to what intuition told her. So if she felt misled and betrayed, hadn't she been the perpetrator as much as he had? Hadn't she betrayed not only herself but *him also?* Wasn't she as guilty as he of avoidance and deception while his well-being hung in the balance?

She realized that she was standing above and apart from him and moved to her knees beside him, placed one hand on his arm and ran her other hand lightly across his forehead to smooth his hair back from his brow. Despite his having been outside for so long in the cold his forehead was damp with sweat. "I'm sorry, Tom. I should have been more involved."

He opened his eyes and gazed earnestly at her through squinting, narrowed lids, his eyebrows arched together. *"You* have nothing to be sorry for. I *lied* to you. You have every right to be angry."

His nostrils flared and he gritted his teeth again but he did not close his eyes against the wave of pain this time.

She stroked the side of his face. "Where does it hurt?"

"In the bones, deep down. Back, hips..." his voice trailed off as he closed his eyes once more.

"Would it help if I massaged it some?"

He shook his head.

She could see that he was beginning to go inward into himself and could no longer sustain conversation, so she tried to make him as comfortable as possible by putting a pillow under his legs and covering him with a blanket. "Can I do anything else to make it easier on you, sweetheart?"

He shook his head again, this time almost imperceptibly, and then turned it toward the backrest of the couch. She did not know if it was the pain or a sense of shame and humiliation or perhaps a combination of all of it, but for now he had moved away from her, and all she could do was stay by his side and pray that the medication would begin to take effect soon. Beyond that, she resolved that she would not make the mistake again of allowing so much free range to his pride or his fear or whatever it was that had kept him from including her in his orbit. And she would not ignore what her own instincts told her. The question now was, what were her instincts telling her? How could she determine what she felt when her heart swung wildly from pie-in-the-sky optimism one moment to all-is-lost pessimism the next? The answer was there *were* no answers yet that she could trust, although she believed she would find them eventually. In the meantime some things were becoming clear. She would not call an ambulance right now—she would wait a bit longer to see if the medication gave him relief. If it did, she would contact Dr. Marshall herself tomorrow assuming his office was open following the holiday, and she would make it understood that from now on she needed to be involved in everything that had to do with her husband's health. And she would brook no argument from either the doctor or Tom about this. If the medication did *not* take effect pretty soon, she would call the ambulance, even against Tom's protestations. She did not feel comfortable trying to drive him to the emergency room herself in this weather even if she *could* get him into the car and out of the driveway, which was highly unlikely, and the alternative of having him remain here indefinitely while she stood by and watched him suffer was no alternative at all. She could not do that, *would* not do that, and she knew that he would not either if their situations were reversed. She would also have to call Ben at some point and let him know what was happening, not only because she felt it was his right to know and because he would want to know, but also because she *needed* to have him know. He was too deeply a part of her life, of *their* lives, and of all her thoughts and considerations of the future not to be kept informed of something so important. And she sensed, also, that she would have to rely upon him for things she could not yet identify.

Cancer, she thought. *My God.*

She realized that she had dozed into sleep when she awoke in her chair to the sound of Tom's moans. *Just past midnight,* she noted by the clock as she moved to his side, thinking, *less than two hours. Double the dosage and less than two hours.*

"Tom," she whispered.

Only a few coals remained of the fire she had started in the fireplace earlier, but in the dim light of the lamp she could see that his eyes were closed and his brow glistened with sweat. "Tom," she whispered again. "Can you hear me?"

He nodded but did not open his eyes.

"I'm going to call an ambulance."

He nodded again and she went to the phone and made the call. On her way back to the living room she glanced outside and noticed that it had stopped snowing, although she could not tell if sleet or freezing rain had begun to fall. Then she remembered the snow blower and decided that it was in the way and she had better try to move it before the ambulance came.

"The ambulance should be here in a few minutes," she told Tom as she knelt down beside him. "I'm just going to step outside for a bit, make sure they find the place okay. Do you need anything before I go?"

He whispered out something that sounded like "new body," and she smiled at him, although his eyes remained shut.

"I'll be right back," she said, and as she got up and moved away from him and began to dress herself to go back outside into the cold she thought again of the word—*cancer*—and of all the people she had known who had had it and of how many of them had died from it.

Not Tom, she thought. *Please, God. Not Tom.*

Chapter Seven

A Simple Request

When the phone startled him early Friday morning Ben was already up grading papers so that he would have the rest of the day free. He picked up the phone before it could finish one ring hoping it would not wake Marie or Teddy and wondering who could be calling so early on the day after Thanksgiving.

"Hello."

"Ben, I'm sorry to call so early. I hope I didn't wake you, but I thought you would want to know right away that your father is in the hospital. I held off calling until I thought you might be awake."

"I've been up grading papers for more than an hour, Mom, but that doesn't matter. What happened? Where are you now?" Worry flooded through him instantly. *Did he have a heart attack? Is he dying?*

"I'm at the hospital, outside his room. He's finally asleep so I didn't want to call from inside the room. Last night he collapsed from back pain while he was out snow blowing. You know how he is, wouldn't wait until morning, insisted he had to get out before the snow turned to rain. I found him outside on his knees and it was all we could do to get him back in the house. He didn't want to go to the hospital so I held off as long as I could, but the pain just wouldn't go away and I finally called an ambulance."

He could sense the uncertainty and self-doubt behind her words. "Sounds like you did the only thing you could do, Mom, under the circumstances." He pushed the curtain aside and looked out the window. When he had awakened earlier it was dark and he could not see clearly how much snow had fallen, but now there was enough light to see there was a good deal of it outside—more than predicted, by the looks of it—although the precipitation had stopped and it did not appear they had received any sleet or rain. It registered in him as a distant and peripheral observation that the snow covering the rooftops and the trees and the barren ground, however early in the season it might be for so much of it, was still a thing of beauty, a thing his father would appreciate if he weren't in the hospital—*and if he hadn't been taken there by ambulance.* "I know he's sleeping now, but how does he seem? How's he taking it?"

"I'm not sure, but I don't think he was upset about the ambulance. He was in too much pain. If anything, he might have been relieved."

Relieved. "Mom, what's going on? What do you think the problem is? This can't really be just arthritis."

"I..." his mother began, but immediately fell silent.

"I'm sorry. You don't have to answer that now. I'll be over right away and we can talk about it then."

There was a long pause. "Mom, are *you* okay?"

"I'm fine, Ben." In her words and in the pause that followed he could hear her gathering herself in to present a stoic front. "Just a little...confused, that's all."

"I'll be right over. Bye, Mom."

"Room 219, Ben. Oh...Ben?"

"Yes?"

"Congratulations. Marie told me the good news last night."

"Thanks, Mom. Does Dad know too?"

"Not yet. I never had a chance to tell him."

"Well maybe that will cheer him up."

"I'm sure it will."

"See you soon."

"Bye, Ben."

He went into the bedroom and saw in the morning twilight that Marie was awake, her eyes searching him for an explanation. "My father is in the hospital," he said in a quiet subdued voice. "He had to be taken there by ambulance last night because of his back."

Marie's brow furrowed with concern. "He seemed fine when he was with us."

"He *was* fine, but then he went out with the snow blower and my mother found him outside on his knees and had to help him back to the house. He was hardly able to *move.*"

"That doesn't sound good."

"No, it doesn't sound good at all. And I don't trust this bullshit about arthritis. Something else is going on and I don't think he's being up front with us about it. The thing is, my mother hasn't mentioned anything else, and I don't think she'd lie to us or try to keep us in the dark about something so important."

"Maybe she doesn't know either."

"That's possible, I guess. I'd be pretty pissed off if it were true, though. He's got no right to keep his own family guessing—especially my mother."

Marie gazed at him in thoughtful silence, and he went over and sat on the edge of the bed beside her. He placed his hand on her belly and made a gentle circling motion, then leaned over to kiss her softly on the lips. "I'd better go now. I want to see how he's doing...and I think my mother could use the support. She sounded a little unsure of things. I'll try not to be gone long."

"Take as long as you need. We'll be fine. And tell your dad we're thinking of him."

"I will. And I'll try to get a few answers, too."

"I hope you do."

Before he left, he looked in on Teddy, who was still sleeping soundly. "Sleep well, my sweet boy," he whispered, "I'll be home as soon as I can."

At the hospital he found his father hooked up to an IV still asleep and his mother dozing in a chair near the bed, though she roused and got up to hug him when he approached.

"I'm glad you're here," she whispered. "Thank you for coming so quickly."

"Has he woken up at all?" he whispered in return.

They kept their voices soft and quiet as they spoke.

"No, thank God. He needs the sleep. Last night was pretty rough on him."

"It must have been rough on you, too."

"I'm okay. Just worried about your father." She gestured toward a chair nearby and said, "Why don't pull up that chair and sit down with me."

Ben did as she asked and then scanned the room. It was a semi-private but the other bed was unoccupied. Everything about the room was predictably institutional, the bland bare walls, the smells of starched sheets and bleach, the predominance of the color white and of glistening chrome, the whirs and clicks of machinery that could not be seen, the TV's situated for convenient distraction. He had never in his life had to spend a night in a hospital, and he hoped that he never would. The only redeeming feature in what he saw was a window to the side of his father that looked out on a small grove of pine trees draped in new snow and lit up by the early morning sun.

His father appeared to be resting easily, his breathing even and rhythmic, but there was something disquieting to Ben about seeing him this way. Lying here in a hospital bed he looked older and even more haggard than he had just a couple of months ago when they had fished together. Granted, he was asleep, but there was a kind of lassitude or helplessness about him, or maybe a kind of vulnerability that Ben had never seen in him before. He had seen it in others in the hospital, this diminishing of a person's life force, but he had not expected to see it in his father. Maybe it was what the hospital did to you, blanched and drained you with its ubiquitous too-bright fluorescent lights, sucked blood and marrow from your being and turned you into a denizen of its own, a pale etiolated creature clad only in the flimsy standard-issue Johnny—with a vague anemic physical resemblance to your former self but with little resemblance to what was most essential and vital about you. You might ultimately get better, as people obviously did in hospitals, but it would not be without paying a price, more personal than financial. There ought to be a sign with a disclaimer near the front desk where all the indignities began: *PAYMENT TERMS: Payment of pride is expected at the time of service. No Exceptions. No Refunds.*

"So how is it that he's come to this, Mom?" he said at last, keeping his voice muted and low. "There *must* be more to it than arthritis. Could he possibly have a disc problem? Did you ever talk with the doctor yourself?"

"No." She lowered her eyes.

"What is it? What do you not want to tell me?"

She was reluctant to speak, and when she did her eyes were downcast, with only an occasional glance up at him. She spoke so softly he almost couldn't hear her. "I probably shouldn't say anything, especially when he's not awake to hear it or defend himself...I feel like I'm betraying him somehow. But after what happened last night I also think it's time to start facing whatever is wrong with him openly." She paused to collect herself and took a deep breath before lifting her gaze to look at him with unwavering steadiness. "Your father *did* go to see Doctor Marshall and he *was* prescribed medication for pain relief that has helped him, at least until last night. But he hasn't had x-rays taken yet and he hasn't had a biopsy done either. The doctor wanted him to do both."

"Because he suspected cancer."

She nodded.

"Damn him!" He shook his head. "How stupid!" He could feel his heart instantly begin to throb, his whole body filling with adrenaline as if he had just been physically assaulted with no warning. It was all he could do to keep his voice down. "Why? Why would he do such a stupid thing?"

She pursed her lips and shook her head.

"And you didn't know anything about it?"

She shook her head again. "Not until last night. But Ben, please, try not to be too hard on him. I know how you feel, I felt the same way myself at first when I found out, but we need to move past that now. We can't go back and undo what's been done. Who knows why he did what he did, or what we would do if faced with the same situation. Maybe he was afraid. Maybe he thought somehow he was protecting us."

"Or maybe he thought he could control it."

"Ben," she said, chastening him with her eyes and the soft abruptness of her voice. There was sorrow and pain and uncertainty in her expression.

"I'm sorry."

"He's going to need you now, even though he may not want to admit it."

"I know. It's just that sometimes he does things I don't understand—like this, hiding the truth about his condition. It infuriates me for some reason. And I can't talk with him the way I can talk to you. I've never been able to."

She looked at him thoughtfully and said with quiet conviction, "You used to be the best of buddies when you were little. And I can tell you this with complete certainty: there's no father that loves his son more than he loves you. That's been true since the day you were born, and it's as true now as it was then."

"Well I guess he just has a strange way of showing it," he said, but the steam was beginning to dissipate from his anger. He watched curiously as a smile, at once patronizing and loving, curled from her lips.

"You're too much alike, you two. Both stubborn and headstrong."

She held his gaze for a moment longer and then looked over at her husband, wondering silently, *What do we do now, my dear Tom? What do we do now?*

"So where do we go from here?" Ben whispered, as if he had been reading her thoughts. "I assume he'll have the x-rays taken right away and then have a biopsy scheduled as soon as possible."

"They've already taken the x-rays. That's one of the first things they did after we got here. As for the biopsy, I guess we'll need to talk with Dr. Marshall about that."

"I think we need to talk with Dr. Marshall *period.* Enough of this groping around for answers and being kept in the dark. I'll also start doing some research on my own. There's an amazing amount of information online."

"That would be good, Ben, I'd appreciate that. Right now I'd be happy just to get answers to some very simple questions. That's not too much to ask, is it?"

"I'd say it's your *right,* Mom. The real question is whether or not they *have* any answers. What did the x-rays show?"

"I don't know yet. We told the Emergency Room doctor about your father's visits to Dr. Marshall, and I got the impression that unless the x-rays showed something that needed to be treated immediately, we should speak to Dr. Marshall about the results."

"Well that's fine, but is Marshall available today?"

"I don't know."

Ben stood up and said, "I'll find out right now. We've done enough waiting. It's time we started getting some answers. I'll be back soon."

"Where are you going?"

"Just out to make a couple of phone calls and talk to some people. I won't be gone long."

"Ben." He stopped and waited. "Just remember that none of this is Dr. Marshall's fault."

"I know that," he said in a soft, measured voice, and then turned and left the room.

When he returned his father was awake and his mother had pulled her chair nearer to his side. His father was sitting up a bit, propped back against the pillows, his hands resting motionless on either side of his torso, but the fact that his eyes were open and alert and his head moved to follow Ben into the room gave Ben the optimistic sense that maybe things were not as bad as he had made them out to be earlier.

"Well, well," his father said.

"So what's this all about, old man?" Ben said, moving closer to shake his father's hand. "I thought you didn't like hospitals." His father took the proffered hand and covered it in both of his own for a moment, a gesture Ben found unusual and oddly comforting.

"I just needed to reconfirm it." He held onto Ben's hand a moment longer. "I hear you have some good news."

"Has Mom told you?"

He released Ben's hand. "Only that you have good news, and it wasn't that you're here to see me."

"Thanks a lot, Mom."

"I never said anything of the sort. You two are terrible."

"Come on, Ben, fess up. What's going on?" A bit of color had come back into his father's wan cheeks.

"Marie is pregnant. She's due sometime early in July."

"Well that *is* good news."

"I meant to tell you last night but I never had the chance."

"Ah, last night," his father said with a wry smile. "A lot of things didn't go as planned last night, wouldn't you say, Fran?"

His mother gave a pensive nod but did not say anything.

"Teddy will have a buddy now. Does he know yet?"

"No, we didn't want to tell him so soon. We'd like to wait until it becomes a little more obvious, so that when we tell him it will be more real to him."

"Makes sense."

They were all silent for a long moment, digesting in their particular ways the confounding notion that such a joyful prospect could present itself in the face of Tom's being taken by ambulance to the hospital.

It was Ben who finally broke the silence. "How are you doing?" he asked, looking squarely into his father's eyes. He could see weariness lurking there behind the recent levity. "Mom said last night was pretty rough."

"Much better now. I'd like to get out of here though. Flattered as I am that you've come, I'd rather not be meeting this way."

Ben smiled and said, "While I was out just now I had a chance to speak with Dr. Marshall on the telephone. He *is* working in his office today, Mom, and he said he'd look at the x-rays right away." She nodded her understanding and thanks.

"Dad, he also said he wants you to have a biopsy done as soon as possible. He obviously didn't want to say too much to me, but he sounded adamant about that."

His father's expression hardened into something grim and somber. "Who appointed you director of protocol for my health?" He looked from Ben to Fran as though he had uncovered a conspiracy.

"It's my fault, Tom," his mother said before he could even begin to construct a response. She spoke with the kind of self-assured authority that would admit no apology. "I told him what's happened because I believe he has a right to know. He's your son, your only child, and after last night I think it's time to put an end to guessing and speculation. It's not fair to push us out of your life when something difficult comes along. If you think I'm wrong, Tom, I'm sorry, but I don't think I am. We're a part of your life, and you're a central part of ours, and that means we want to know what's going on. We *need* to know."

"But it's *my life.*" His father looked at each of them in turn, his expression stern and uncompromising. "Do you understand that?"

Ben did understand that, and respected it as well, though he found himself thinking of John Donne's perfect retort, which he also believed and respected—*No man is an island*—even as his mother was speaking again, her voice sympathetic and controlled. As he listened it occurred to him that it was clearly best, at least for now, if he deferred to her. She was in full command of herself and of the moment.

"We do," his mother said. "But I don't think that gives you the right to conduct it as if our concerns don't exist. Do you?"

His father continued to gaze at her, silent and unyielding at first, but then turned toward the window that looked out upon the grove of snow-laden pine trees. The wind was apparently beginning to pick up because the branches of the trees were swaying and wispy clouds of snow occasionally dropped away from boughs released of their tension. The furrows of his father's brow relaxed. His father took a deep breath and exhaled slowly.

"No."

A nurse breezed in to check his father's IV and said, "How are you feeling, Mr. Derringer? Are you still feeling any pain?" She wore green scrubs and her dark hair was pulled back into a tight bun. She was thin and pretty, but the features of her face were sharp, angular.

"No," his father said. "The pain seems to be under control. I'm just a little tired right now."

"Well maybe you should try to get some more sleep." She glanced meaningfully at Ben and his mother.

"We'll leave him alone for a while," his mother said.

"I didn't mean for you to leave," the nurse said, although Ben knew that was *exactly* what she meant.

"That's all right," his mother said. "We'll come back later."

Ben could not tell for sure, but it seemed to him that his father's words implied something more than lack of sleep.

Tom felt relieved when they left, which struck him as peculiar given that he was in a place he had always loathed—a hospital bed—and having his family around was a source of cheer. But it was also, in part, a source of his discomfort. Their leaving took some of the pressure away, relieved him of the weight of being on display. *Here he is, folks, the man who's been hospitalized for pain. Let's see how he's dealing with it now.* He hated to be seen this way, in a weakened condition, reduced to having a tube stuck in his arm because he couldn't manage the pain himself.

Pressure. As he drifted back into sleep once more he thought again of how for all of his adult life and perhaps even extending back into his early teenage years, beneath the surface of daily living with all its attendant masks and guises he had regarded life as an unrelenting source of pressure. It had occurred to him forcefully once when he was out driving alone at night on a dark and lonely road and being tailgated by a tractor-trailer: the pressure was like that, like the headlights so bright and near and blinding in your rearview mirror they seemed to be coming from in front of you, and the source of their light, the massive truck itself, ready to roll right over or through you if you hesitated for even an instant. *Pressure.* Pressure to conform to others' demands and expectations—to be aggressive when you were by nature shy, to move faster when you wanted to move slowly, to be social when you preferred to be alone. Pressure to wake up at a designated time and to dress in a certain kind of clothing and to be punctual for the obligations and appointments of the day. Why else, in all honesty, had he left the security of the architectural firm so many years ago and set out to fend for himself if not out of a response to such pressure, trading the pressure of others' expectations for the pressure of owning his own business, of staking his family's well being to his personal, individual success or failure? Pressure to be smiling and positive when you did not feel that way, when what you saw was a world in which the dark side of life—not just calamity and accident and misfortune, not just natural disaster, but deliberate, senseless human cruelty—presented enough evidence of mayhem and enough of an argument against some divine order or plan to undermine all but the most irrational faith. Pressure to *live:* witness the effect of trying to commit suicide by drowning—you couldn't keep yourself submerged long enough to suck in water and end it all because the survival instinct, the *pressure to live* was too strong, and so if you were intent on dying you had to do it in a way that would circumvent that pressure, quickly and violently, as with a gun or a leap from a cliff, or with deceptive simplicity, as with an overdose of something so easy to swallow it didn't seem you could possibly be doing anything harmful to yourself. Pressure from the *outside:* from all the sacred precepts and traditions regarding the sanctity of life and all the taboos against suicide that dated back to the beginning of recorded human history and that were inculcated from birth into each new generation, and from the proliferation of teeming ubiquitous life in every spring of every year—the ceaseless twittering of birds and the relentless importuning choruses of peepers like the imperative voice of life itself, at once announcing its omnipresence and issuing its devastatingly simple injunction: *live, and make new life;* and pressure from the *inside:* from the smallest to the largest of cells dividing and multiplying and repairing damaged tissue and attacking invaders and fighting to maintain the body's safety and wholeness and immunity from disease, laboring ceaselessly and invisibly night and day with the implacable and peremptory insistence of an automaton to keep lungs breathing oxygen and heart pumping blood, to transport food to the farthest reaches of the body and to stir the libido through scent and sound and touch to act upon its charge to procreate. And even more, beyond the irresistible pressure, the external and internal conspiracy enjoining one to live, there was the pressure to *honor* living, to *celebrate* life, to lavish the highest praise on the ineluctable fact of existence as though it were a *choice,* as though it were merely one possibility, the best one, among a wide range of options, when in reality there were only two options so far as anyone knew, to live or not to live, and who knew what it meant *not to live?* Who had the right to pass judgment upon it? Despite the most profound speculations of the finest philosophical and religious minds over the entire course of history, no one could say with certainty what it meant not to live. We knew only what it meant to live, and even then we did not really know what it meant to live because we could not measure it against the alternative of not living. And so like frightened children afraid of the dark and the unknown we had constructed the foundation of our universe out of what we thought we knew of living and had denounced what we thought we knew of not living.

But there was now inside him the force of the not-living, or the anti-living, the cancer, which he knew he had, the biopsy would be a mere formality, and he wondered if in some twisted fashion he had brought the cancer on himself. Had he not respected life enough during his time on earth, not shown enough gratitude or proper deference? Had he been an insurrectionist in his thinking, a subversive, a heretic? *Had he wished for death?* Was he being punished and humbled now for his failure to appreciate what he had, for his sin of pride? If so, he would apologize to whomever or whatever he could, for he had meant no harm, he *loved* life also, wanted most assuredly to continue living, but he did not want the pain. He would deal with what he must, with all the continual and myriad and inescapable forms of pressure, but he did not want the pain. If it came down to it he would trade years of his life in exchange for living pain free. He did not need to live to be a hundred, or even eighty. (How peculiar it was to be thinking in these terms now, when the end of life was beginning to come clearly into view, when looking twenty years ahead—which was all he could reasonably do given his age—in all likelihood encompassed the end of his life, the countdown of years beginning in earnest, and yet he could so easily account for twenty years backward into the past. How was it that he had come to this point so quickly? How was it that he had grown so old so fast? Where had all the years gone?) He would accept merely living to seventy, or even sixty-five (did he really believe this? could he really be thinking this? only *five years?)* if he could be assured of not having to deal with the pain.

There was much he could do in five years if he knew that he could live them without being crippled—a lifetime could be packed into five years, an intensity of feeling and activity and awareness built into every year, every month, every week. And so what if his newly won retirement *(how long was it now...less than a year still? so what if that was another kind of betrayal?)* would have to be curtailed sooner than he thought? At least he would be retired, and he and Fran would have time to spend with their grandchildren and to travel and to do more of the charitable work he had never had quite enough time for when he was working full time. He had often thought he'd like to hook on with Habitat for Humanity and put his skills to work there helping to design and build houses, creating something that would give lasting aid to families that had been less fortunate than he had been in his lifetime. And there would be plenty of time to teach Teddy—and maybe even his new grandchild, boy *or* girl—how to grow vegetables in a garden and how to cast a fly line and how to tell the difference between a brook trout and a rainbow trout, and maybe in a few years to watch Teddy play in a baseball game on one of those lovely soft green evenings in May when nothing could be better than to watch kids playing ball. There would be plenty of time to do all that he needed to do in order to leave gracefully...if only he could do so without pain. That was the deal he would be willing to make.

But then it occurred to him that maybe he was being a bit premature here, maybe he was getting ahead of himself. Yes, in all likelihood he had cancer inside him—he could feel it, he *knew* it—but he did not know how serious it was, how treatable it might turn out to be, how many years he might be able to finagle out of the situation. Maybe five years was cutting himself way too short. Maybe if he were willing to accept *some* pain, nothing too overwhelming, but *some,* especially in the short-term, he could buy another five or *ten* years. Maybe...(he was reluctant to even think this) what he had was curable and there would be no need to make a deal at all. That was possible. Anything was possible. He would just have to wait and see, but it couldn't hurt to have a plan. It couldn't hurt to have thought it through a bit and to have his request ready if the need arose. The only problem was, to whom did you put in your request?

He could feel himself floating just a bit and wondered if he was awake or merely dreaming. He did not know, could not tell for sure, but he felt weightless, buoyant, unattached to his physical body, and although when he tried to open his eyes he found that he could not, he was aware of a bright suffusion of light as though he were drifting through banks of brightly lit clouds, like those uppermost mushrooming towers of cumulonimbus clouds that you could sometimes see lit up by the sun, except that now he was not viewing them from a distance but from the inside, drifting, somnolent, content to be free of gravity and pain. It *was* a problem, though, whom to ask. The doctor? The doctor had no more control than any lay person, really. God? He had dismissed all notions of a compassionate ruler of the universe long ago as nothing more than the misguided wishful thinking of those desperate for something to believe in. The evidence to the contrary was staggering, overwhelming. So if not the doctor and not God, whom? Or what? Was there some sort of *life force*—not even necessarily conscious—that monitored all living things and that could detect and eliminate that which through its deviation threatened life, just as immune cells in the body identified, attacked, and destroyed dangerous viruses and bacteria? If this were so, how did he go about pleading his case? How did he convince this unconscious power that he was reformed, and from now on would pay due homage to all things living, including his own life? Or was it to himself that he should be properly making amends? If he had brought the cancer upon himself, could he not also take it away, or reverse the momentum he had somehow unwittingly begun? *I will think only good and positive thoughts if I can spare myself this ordeal that I don't want.* I don't want. *That was the key, really. I don't want this misery. Truly.* I DON'T WANT IT!

But he knew that if he had brought it on himself he had done so at a level beneath what he was conscious of, and therein lay the true treachery. The physical war within him—being waged with such ferocity and yet so deeply hidden from view as to be invisible—was merely the outermost indicator, the corporeal symptom that suggested an even more pitched battle going on somewhere else, against a traitorous part of himself lurking below conscious awareness, a battle he was losing without knowing why he was losing it or when it had begun or even why it was being fought, though the stakes were clear: life or death. But with every fiber of his conscious being he wanted to live, there was too much in his life for him to live for to think or feel otherwise, and he surely did not want any of the pain he had had to endure. So how was it that this was happening to him? How was it that the renegade within had been able to thwart all that he loved of life by perpetrating such a deception upon him, by allowing this anti-life to grow and thrive undetected for so long inside him? *WHY* WAS IT HAPPENING?

I will fight it, he thought, as if in answer, *and you, now that I know.* And then the plea went out, to whomever or whatever, to himself or to no one at all, *Just give me time.* Simply and without anguish: *Just give me time.*

When he awoke again he saw that Fran and Ben had returned and were sitting in the chairs they had been in before. "I'm sorry," he said.

"For what, Tom?" Fran said gently. "You have nothing to apologize for."

"For all of this. For last night. For the two of you having to be here. For thinking only of myself and not letting you know what's going on. And then for getting angry with you both when all *you're* doing is trying to help me, trying to save me from myself. There's a lot I need to apologize for."

She smiled tolerantly. "Well, my dear, as far as I'm concerned it's all water over the dam now. The important thing is for us to find out what's wrong and get you well."

"I agree," Ben said. His aspect was more severe than his mother's, but he had the same blue eyes Tom had always loved so well in both of them, the same wavy hair and clear high forehead that bespoke a kind of openness and integrity. The resemblance was strong between mother and son.

"I'm ready to do whatever I need to do. I don't want to fool around any more. If it's cancer I've got, then I want to know that and start fighting it. I feel like I've been wasting time—yours *and* mine—and life's too short, time's too precious, to waste any more of it."

For the first time since he had initially learned of his father's problems Ben could hear in his father's voice a serious regard for the need to winnow out the truth, buttressed by a sense of resolve that had been entirely misdirected until now. The tiredness he had heard only a short while ago seemed to have disappeared, or to have been replaced by the sort of stubborn energy Ben had always seen as a fundamental character trait in his father. But despite the encouragement he felt, he could not dispel an eerie and unsettling feeling that had come over him the instant he remembered the line from RICHARD II that his father's words had triggered in him: *I wasted time, and now time doth waste me.*

"That's good to hear, Dad. That's really good to hear."

Chapter Eight

A Battery of Tests

Dr. Marshall looked at the x-rays for Tom Derringer and saw what he had suspected following the rectal exam, the results of the PSA test and Tom's own description of the back pain he had been experiencing. But what he saw was even worse than he had feared: the evidence of bone damage was significant and *widespread.* No wonder Tom had been complaining of pain. The thought occurred to him now as he looked at the films, feeling suddenly very tired this day after Thanksgiving, that it would have been better if he had given himself and his staff today off as a holiday also. Then at least he would have had a long weekend free before having to confront Tom with what he had found. But it was a selfish thought, and he dismissed it quickly. It was better for Tom that they begin to understand the likely reason for his pain and get on top of it as quickly as possible. They would have to get the results of a biopsy and run more tests, of course, but he did not hold out much hope for what they would find. God only knew what was in store for Tom Derringer, but the choices he would probably have to make and the path of his life in the foreseeable future were not things to be wished upon anyone. *Poor bastard,* he thought. *Poor helpless bastard.* And then he pondered for a moment how we are all of us, from a certain perspective, poor helpless bastards, but he did not like to go too far in that direction and abruptly took the x-rays down, put them away, and switched off the view screen light.

After learning that Dr. Marshall had called the hospital and was planning to stop in to visit with his father sometime after 4:30, Ben went home for a few hours to be with Marie and Teddy. The doctor had left instructions that his father was to have a bone scan done right away and that he be held overnight so that he could be monitored and then have further tests done in the morning, which was apparently what the doctor wanted to discuss with his father. Ben had no intention of missing this meeting, but the annual Christmas parade was scheduled for this afternoon and he had been hyping it up to Teddy for the past week, promising Santa would be there along with fire trucks and marching bands and big floats ("What's a float, Daddy?" Teddy had asked) and horses and clowns and maybe, if Teddy was a really good boy all week, there would be some candy for him at the parade too. He could hardly beg off such a time with his son, and so he hurried back to the hospital afterwards hoping that he would not be too late to meet the doctor.

He had to drive with his headlights on now, and he lamented as he did every year the way daylight diminished so quickly by the end of November. It was a peculiar time of year, filled with paradoxes and abrupt mood swings, as though the foreshortened days had the effect of compressing and thereby accentuating everything (he had read somewhere that many merchants did 70%-80% of their business for the year in the six week period leading up to Christmas). Despite the too-intense Christmas fervor which kicked into high gear after Thanksgiving, and despite the obscene spread of commercialism—which had seemed in recent years to extend further and further back in time like some insidious disease, back into early November and even October—he genuinely liked this time of year. He liked the coming together of family and friends, the abundance—and frequency—of good food and drink, the heightened sense of cheer in most people you met on the street, he even liked all the Christmas decorations and lights (garish though some of them could be at times) and the way the city glittered as though it were itself an enormous shining gift. He knew it could be argued—and he had made the argument himself more than once—that people's efforts were largely misguided, as most people relied almost exclusively upon material things to communicate what they felt, to show their love and affection through *objects,* and that many people tried *too* hard to make everything come out right, which led to much of the season's gross surfeits and sorrowful disappointments, but it was as though beneath all the excesses and facades and hurly-burly, for this one time of year, at least, people sincerely *tried* to be happy and generous, to get along with each other, *yearned* for something more than pretense. And yet it was a sad time also, a time when life seemed to close down more every day as the circle of darkness tightened around it, and he could sympathize with those people whose sorrow and despair *in*creased as the amount of daylight *de*creased. Viewed from this perspective, all the festivities of light and sound seemed to have about them an air of desperation, as though at their core, their truest source, the intent was not so much to celebrate life as to fend off the night.

At the hospital he was pleased to find that the doctor had not yet arrived. He told his mother and father about the parade and how excited Teddy was to see Santa, although he had been a little frightened by the loud air horn blasts from all the fire trucks heralding Santa's arrival. "The poor little guy was trembling and teary one minute, pressing his hands tight to his ears, and then beaming the next minute, bouncing in my arms and calling out to Santa as loud as he could. Marie and I were convinced he would have left us and gone away with Santa if I hadn't had such a tight grip on him."

"I'm sorry we missed it," his father said. "Believe me, I'd much rather have been out there with all of you."

"Well, the neat thing is he's at that age when everything is new and magical and there's no thought of disbelief. Hopefully that'll last for a *few* years, Dad."

They were all silent after that, and in a while Dr. Marshall came in and shook Tom's hand and asked how he was feeling.

"Not bad at all," Tom said, and then introduced his wife and son to the doctor. "I wouldn't mind getting out of here though."

"That's why I wanted to see you," the doctor said. He was standing near Tom at the side of the bed, his arms extending down before him with one hand on the other below his waist. His head was slightly inclined toward one side, his expression solemn. "I've had a chance to look over the x-rays," he said, pausing and glancing at Fran and Ben.

"It's all right," Tom said. A faint wry smile curled from his lips. "They can be trusted, I think."

The doctor nodded but directed his words to Tom. "Tom, the x-rays show considerable bone damage to the lower area of your spine, your hips, and your pelvic bones, but there's nothing that looks like a new fracture, which means that the pain you experienced last night was not the result of any trauma that just happened recently. You undoubtedly aggravated the problem last night, but the damage was not sustained last night."

"Then what caused it?"

The question hung there for a moment as if he had thrown out a live grenade the doctor did not want to touch.

"I don't want to get too far ahead of ourselves here," the doctor said equivocally. "Without the biopsy, I'm reluctant to make any sort of definitive diagnosis. That's why I'd like to have the biopsy done first thing in the morning."

"But you don't think it's arthritis," Tom said, wanting clarity. He no longer had any use for evasions or obfuscation. "You think it's cancer."

"Unfortunately, that's what the indications are at this point. But I'd like to gather more information before saying much more, and I'd like to consult with an oncologist as well."

"You think the cancer has spread to Tom's bones?" Fran blurted out, suddenly alarmed. She did not know much about prostate cancer but she knew what it meant if cancer had spread to the bones. She had watched Alice Goodwin, one of her dearest friends, die an agonizingly difficult death just a few years ago after Alice's breast cancer had spread to her bones.

The doctor hesitated. This was, indeed, the most difficult part of his profession, and there were times, such as now, when he would rather be anything else but a doctor. "It's a possibility that cancer has metastasized to the bones, but again, until we get results from the biopsy it would be best if we waited to draw any conclusions." He looked from Fran to Ben and then back to Tom. "I only wanted to stop by and explain the rationale for keeping you here, Tom, and to emphasize how important it is to have the biopsy done right away."

Tom realized they all knew he had avoided having the procedure done sooner, although the doctor probably had no idea that both Fran and Ben knew also. "You don't have to worry about that," he said to Dr. Marshall. "I'm sorry I didn't come in when you first asked me to, but that's over and done with. Right now I need to learn the truth. I *want* to find out what's happening."

"Good. In the meantime, we'll try to keep you as comfortable as possible. I don't want you to hesitate to let me or someone here at the hospital know if you're experiencing pain.

There are always ways to manage pain, so there's no reason for you to be suffering from it needlessly." The doctor reached for Tom's hand and shook it once more. "I'll be speaking to you soon, Tom. Good luck tomorrow morning."

"Thanks," Tom said, trying to gauge from the doctor's eyes whether it was luck he really needed or a miracle, but he could read nothing more than compassion and concern from the doctor's practiced demeanor.

Dr. Marshall nodded to Fran and Ben and then moved quickly out of the room, grateful that the week was done and he had finished this most difficult task and could now go home for a couple of days.

Ben had been wanting to speak to Dr. Marshall for some time now and had hurried to be present for this meeting, yet he had not said a word during the doctor's entire visit. He had stood there and listened like a dumbstruck child, and he felt a bit foolish and ashamed now for having done nothing to support his father. Not that he could have done much. He certainly couldn't have changed the doctor's outlook or altered anything about his father's condition, but to have said nothing made him feel vain and powerless, and underneath that, traitorous, as though he had abandoned his father during a time when his help was most needed. And his continued silence even now, his inability to fashion words out of what he was feeling, humbled him in a way that he had never expected.

"Dr. Marshall seems like a pretty decent guy," Ben said at last.

"I think he is," his father said.

"Do you trust his judgment?"

"I have no reason not to."

They were quiet again for a time, with Fran working diligently to get her mind around what she had just heard. Ever since the realization had dawned upon her that Tom's pain was *bone* pain, and the connection between bone pain and cancer had clicked into place in her mind like the tumbler of a lock, she had felt shaken, and did not trust her voice not to betray her. He had told her just last night that it was deep down, in the bones, and yet she had failed to make the connection even then. Back pain was one thing—everyone had back pain. It was almost fashionable to complain about back pain. But pain in the bones was another thing altogether, and she had neglected it as a possibility. For months now she had been seeing what was happening to him, had known it was serious, had urged him to seek help, but she had not truly paid enough attention to it. She had taken what he had been saying, what she had been seeing, and relegated it to the commonplace, as though it couldn't possibly have been more than that. *I should have known,* she thought, and yet she had not known. *Not even last night. I've failed him again,* she accused herself bitterly, and she wondered if Tom himself understood the significance of what the doctor had said.

"Are you comfortable enough now, Tom?" she asked, and he nodded. "The doctor was very clear about not accepting pain. I liked that."

"I'm fine. But the two of you must be getting hungry and tired. You should go out and get something to eat. Fran, you've been up since the middle of the night and you haven't eaten anything all day. You must be exhausted. And Ben, I appreciate your being here, but you've spent enough time in this place for one day. Why don't you get yourself home and try to enjoy what's left of the evening. Read Teddy a story for me. What was that fishing story we liked so much? You know, the one about the big old trout no one could catch until the young boy did?"

"*UNCLE HUGH,* you mean?"

"That's it, *UNCLE HUGH.* Read him *UNCLE HUGH* for me."

Ben recalled the story of the magnificent fish that not even the best fly fishermen could catch. He had an immediate image of the young boy's intense joy at seeing the fish take his fly, leap high out of the water in a graceful arc, and then smash back down with a powerful jolt to his rod, followed by the boy's confusion and sadness upon bringing in the fish without a fight and discovering that the fish lay there in the water before him lifeless and unmoving. Whereupon the boy remembered the words of his uncle from Scotland, who had fished all around the world but was unable to catch the big trout himself during his visit, *He'll be caught when his time comes.* It was a fine story, though not by any means typical children's fare, dealing as it did with the enduring beauty of the river where the boy lived and the boy's coming to understand the inevitability and naturalness of death and loss.

"I will, Dad," he said, wanting to say more but not at all clear what it was he wanted to say. He moved closer and his father took his hand, as he had done earlier, in both of his own, and again held it longer than usual. "I'll see you at *home,*" Ben said. "Soon."

"Right."

"Good luck tomorrow."

"Thanks, Ben."

He gave his mother a hug and she held him very tightly for a long moment, and when he pulled back and looked into her eyes he could see a kind of fear and vulnerability there that he had rarely seen in her before, not even when her own mother, his grandmother, had died several years ago. "Are you all right, Mom?" he asked, knowing that she was not.

"I'm fine," she said, giving him the lie that she knew he would not believe but that he needed in order to leave. "A little tired, is all."

"Get some rest then, both of you. I'll call tomorrow." His mother nodded and they all said their goodbyes more cheerfully than any of them felt.

As he retraced his route through the brightly lit labyrinthine hallways of the hospital, bulletin boards decorated here and there with the colors and trappings of the Christmas season, the feeling that had been gnawing at the borders of his awareness ever since the doctor had left intensified. But only now was he beginning to understand the nature and significance of that feeling: *it was the feeling of defeat.*

Tom disliked everything about the biopsy: the enema that he was given the night before; the indignity of the position he had to be in for the procedure to be done; the shape and size of the instruments used; and the fact that these instruments, which looked to have been devised by the Marquis de Sade, were used to invade the most private places within him. It was true, as he had been told beforehand, that having the biopsy taken was not a particularly painful procedure, but in a way that was irrelevant. What was relevant was that it had to be done at all, and that as a man who had always taken pride in his fitness and his physical well being, he had been forced to undergo a procedure that he found humiliating. And yet he maintained his equanimity throughout. He thanked the hospital staff (whom he found generally capable and responsive) for any little consideration they showed him (propping pillows for him, asking him about his comfort), and he remained as polite and congenial as if he had been having his teeth cleaned rather than his bowels probed and his prostate snipped.

When it was all finished he was given a prescription to continue the antibiotics he had started taking the night before, and Fran was there to greet him and drive him home, though he insisted on doing that himself. He had had quite enough of feeling helpless and out of control of even the most basic elements of his life.

"How was it, sweetheart?" Fran asked him in the car on the way home. "Were they right about it not being very painful?"

"Yes," he said, embarrassed and not wanting to provide details but remembering again with all-too-sharp clarity the instruments and the position and the uncomfortable sense he had had, while he was being probed and snipped, that his body was no longer his own. It had made him feel, for a brief but powerful moment, a kind of connection to those unfortunate souls who had been victims of Hitler's "medical" experiments in concentration camps, although immediately after thinking this he felt ashamed of himself because the motives involved were so completely different. "It wasn't too bad."

Fran reached over and stroked the side of his face. She knew the procedure must have been difficult for him even if it *hadn't* been painful. "So what happens next?"

"We wait, I guess. I'll get a phone call about the biopsy results when they have them."

He had begun to think quite a bit lately about waiting. All of life, it seemed, was a kind of waiting, or an endless series of waits. When you were a child you couldn't wait to be bigger and you couldn't wait to be a year older and you couldn't wait for summer vacation or Christmas to come, and yet the not wanting to wait never diminished the waiting itself, and almost in the moment when the birthday or Christmas came there was another whole year of waiting beyond it. As a teenager you couldn't wait to turn sixteen so that you could get your driver's license and you couldn't wait to be old enough to drink and you couldn't wait to have sex for the first time, but as in childhood it was the waiting that was the only constant, and the milestones turned out to be chimerical, like the illusion of water that seems always just a bit farther ahead on the sun-baked surface of a macadam highway. Then as a working adult you couldn't wait for vacation to come each year and you couldn't wait to find the right person to marry and you couldn't wait to have children (and then couldn't wait to get them out of diapers and, eventually, out of the house), and when the children were at last adults you couldn't wait to have grandchildren, and you couldn't wait for your portfolio to grow large enough for you to be able to retire and travel. And within all of it, within all the major contexts of not wanting to wait that occurred throughout life, there were countless minor examples of not wanting to wait that occurred virtually every day (couldn't wait for school or work to be over for the day, couldn't wait for Friday to come and the weekend to begin, couldn't wait to see a certain movie), and underpinning all the *not wanting*, comprising the vast majority of our time on earth, was the very thing we did not want, the waiting. It might reasonably be said that life *was* waiting, or at least a lesson in learning to wait. Why, then, did we resist it so much? What was it about waiting that we disliked so thoroughly, or...that we feared? What were we waiting for? For life to begin? For joy? Was that it—the moments we waited for most represented life and joy, and all the time in between those moments represented something other than joy, a kind of fallowness or absence, a void, a kind of death? Did waiting remind us of death, or provide us with the time and the inescapable opportunity to remember that death, after all, was what we were all ultimately waiting for? Was that the test we were forced to take, the question life posed to all of us: *How well can you wait for death?*

"It's very hard," she said, thinking about the possibility that he not only had cancer but that it was within his bones.

"What?"

"The waiting."

"Yes, it is. We don't have much choice about it, though."

She considered this for a moment, searching for a reply that might help them both without sounding hollow, but she could not find it. "It makes you feel so helpless."

He did not answer and they were both silent again for a long while as he drove. They had been married for thirty-five years now, and yet neither knew quite what to say to the other. There was a shyness between them that they both felt, harkening back to their youth, but this time it was not the arousal of sexual passion and the sometimes awkward negotiations of intimacy that constrained them, nor any moral strictures that came from outside them. This time their silence and their discomfort and the quickened beating of their hearts grew out of the respect and love each had for the other, and the dread of separation that was beginning to work its way into their thoughts despite their best efforts to prevent it from happening.

"I'm not very optimistic about this biopsy," he said at last.

"I know," she said. "I'm worried too." She reached over and placed a hand gently on his shoulder.

"It doesn't seem real, somehow. It doesn't seem possible. *Cancer,* for God's sake. No one in my family has ever had cancer. All along I've been worried about dying from a heart attack like my father, and now...."

"But you can't be thinking about dying, Tom," she interrupted. "We don't know anything for sure yet."

"How can I not think about it? If I have cancer and it's in my bones, I'm as good as dead. It's only a matter of time."

So he does understand, she thought. She felt a sudden tightness in her chest and a churning in her stomach. "Don't *say* that. We still need to find out for sure what's wrong."

He turned the car onto the road to their home and checked the rearview mirror, then said, "Be honest with me. Haven't you thought about it?" There was no one behind them and no one coming in the other direction, so he glanced over to look at her for a moment.

She closed her eyes and nodded. "I have, but not much. I don't even want to think of life without you." It was true. She *had* thought about it, but every time the possibility of his dying began to present itself to her she fought it back with all the force of her being. She would simply not give in to such darkness as long as she could still pray, as long as there was still the light of hope.

The weather today was much milder than it had been and he saw that the snow was already beginning to melt and reveal dirty browns banks from all the sand and salt used to treat the roads. He slowed down as he turned into their driveway, passing the point at the end where he had collapsed so short a while ago. In chronological time it was less than forty-eight hours since that had happened, but in real time, that time in which events unfold—outside of our control—and define for us what the future holds, it had happened a lifetime ago.

He eased the car forward into the garage and brought it to a halt, then turned off the ignition. "I think you're right," he said, leaning over to kiss her on the forehead. "I think we still need to find out for sure what's wrong."

In the interim, during the waiting, the pain came back. The new medication he had been given worked better than the previous one, and the pain was not as intense as it had been before he went into the hospital, but it was enough that he did not want to move any more than he had to, and though he tried, he could not hide this from Fran. So they read books and rented videos and watched movies (comedies mostly—he found he had little interest in anything that could be construed as morbid) and bided time. Ben came over once, with Teddy in tow, to share with them some of what he had been discovering about prostate problems—not just prostate cancer—through the Internet. He took great pleasure in seeing his grandson again, but the reams of printouts Ben gave them to look over regarding symptoms and tests and treatments and medications left him feeling tired and overwhelmed. There was too much to digest, it seemed, when the matter was ultimately very simple: Did he or did he not have cancer? And if he did, how could he fight it? How could he have time without pain? How could he live well enough to ski again, or to wade into a river in the spring to catch trout, or tend to his garden with that beautiful little boy, his grandson, beside him? These were the only things that mattered, and the only questions he wanted answers to. The rest was all drivel.

The answer to the first question did turn out to be simple. Just as everyone had begun to assume, he indeed had cancer. The biopsy proved positive, and the bone scan taken in conjunction with the x-rays revealed that the cancer was *widespread* within him, showing up as something called "blastic" growth (the terminology he was learning had already gone way beyond what he had any desire to know) in his pelvic and hip bones, his spine, and in other bone sites as well. In an almost perverse way he welcomed the news for the certainty it provided (there was no longer any speculation about cancer: it was now fact, and he preferred fact over speculation) and for the justification it gave to the pain he had been experiencing. No one could accuse him—nor could he accuse himself—of being a hypochondriac or of having imagined the pain. The pain was *real*, and now they all knew why. On the other hand, the news hit him with devastating force—the certainty of it was also like the certainty of a death sentence. It was as though he were on death row now, with Dr. Marshall serving as his lawyer, and his only hope was to win stays of execution from some unknown judge.

If he found the answer to the first question to be devastatingly simple and certain (he would never forget the doctor's honest, unembellished words over the telephone, "I'm afraid there's no doubt anymore that you do have cancer, Tom"), he found the answers to some of the other questions maddeningly difficult. Shortly after learning the results of the tests, he and Fran met with Dr. Marshall to discuss his prognosis and his options for treatment. The doctor explained to them the whole concept of "staging" the disease (replete with a baggage car's worth of information and terminology he did not want to possess). According to the pathology report, his cancer had been graded a "10" using something called the "Gleason scale." The doctor called it a "Stage D2" cancer or, using another staging method, a "T4N+M+" cancer. What it all meant when the jargon was distilled into laymen's terms was that he had a highly malignant and very aggressive cancer inside him which they needed to begin treating right away. As to the only information he truly wanted to learn, *how much time do I have,* and *what kind of quality of life can I expect,* the doctor was equivocal.

"I can't honestly answer those questions, Tom. They depend on the course of treatment we follow and how the cancer responds to that treatment."

"What *are* the courses of treatment?" Fran asked. "What would you recommend?" She had a pad of legal paper that she scribbled notes on as the doctor talked. Since learning the truth about Tom's condition she had resolved to be fastidious in learning all she could, and helping Tom to stay organized and remember everything they talked about with the doctor. She vowed to herself that she would never fail him again.

"Given what we're dealing with, what makes the most sense is to follow the standard treatment of hormonal therapy. Most of the time hormonal therapy has a marked effect in slowing the cancer's rate of growth, and at the same time it generally provides significant pain relief."

"And what exactly does 'hormonal therapy' mean?" Tom asked warily.

"Well, basically it means reducing the amount of male hormones, or androgens, circulating through your body. About ninety per cent of the time, the cancer cells are sensitive to androgens such as testosterone. In other words, the cancer cells seem to feed off the androgens. So if we reduce the food source, the androgens, we reduce the cancer growth. There's more than one way, though, of accomplishing this reduction."

He had the uncomfortable feeling that even though the doctor was answering their questions, he wasn't really learning anything at all. He felt as though he were in the midst of a jungle, and each step ahead, each new piece of information, instead of helping him break through into a clearing, plunged him deeper into a kind of dark and suffocating entanglement where the more he struggled the tighter he was bound.

They were sitting in the doctor's personal office, where the furniture and the surroundings were cozier and more friendly than in the sterile examination rooms. There was a picture of a pretty young blond woman, presumably the doctor's daughter (although maybe it was his wife?), smiling as she sat atop a chestnut colored horse.

He glanced from Fran, who was still jotting notes with business-like efficiency, to Dr. Marshall, who waited with benign calmness for any questions before pushing ahead into new territory. The doctor was sitting in the swivel chair behind his desk, leaning slightly backward, hands folded low on his lap. "I get the feeling somehow that we're skirting issues here. Like there's something that's not being said that should be said. Am I just imagining things, or what?"

The doctor frowned a bit and leaned further back in his chair. "Well, I'm not sure if I've made it as clear as I perhaps could have that whatever treatment procedure we decide upon is not likely to provide a cure. Given the cancer you have, Tom, the treatment options are primarily palliative in nature." As if realizing the harshness of his message despite the gentleness and sympathy with which he had tried to deliver it, the doctor added, "I'm sorry if I haven't seemed forthright enough about the situation. Believe me, I don't want to sound disingenuous, but on the other hand I also don't want to give the impression there's no hope. Many men with a diagnosis such as yours have lived quite a long time, and with a very good quality of life, through hormonal therapy alone or in conjunction with other treatments."

What he understood from this was as clear as the doctor could possibly have made it without being blunt and cruel: *you're a dead man, and the odds are that it will be sooner rather than later.*

Fran had been listening intently all along as she was writing, fearing the worst and hoping for the best, but when she heard the doctor's last words she latched onto them as someone drowning might latch onto a lifeline. "So even though hormonal therapy might not provide a cure, it could keep Tom's cancer from growing for many years?" she said, gazing directly into the doctor's eyes.

"Yes, it's possible." The doctor was looking at Fran and nodding as though he had found an ally in her. "There's no guarantee, of course, but it is possible."

He continued to have that gnawing, persistent feeling that something wasn't being said, as though despite all the bad news, he still hadn't heard the worst. But he wondered what could possibly be worse than a death sentence, especially when the doctor had assured him that pain could always be managed. "What's involved in the *options* you referred to?"

The doctor leaned forward in his chair, his eyes momentarily focused on the picture of the young woman on the horse. His hands came to rest on the edge of the desk, as though to keep himself from pitching too far forward. He looked at Tom again, but the steadiness and compassion in his eyes could not mask the difficult negotiation of thoughts into words. "There are a few different options, Tom. Probably the simplest and most effective is a type of surgery called a bilateral orchiectomy, which involves removal of the testicles. This procedure almost entirely eliminates the production of testosterone, and as a result, it's usually very effective in slowing cancer growth and reducing pain."

Tom was silent as the doctor described more of the advantages as well as the disadvantages of this procedure and then went on to explain other options such as the use of anti-hormonal agents like "LHRH agonists" and something else called "estrogen therapy," each of which, like the surgery, could prolong his life but could also involve some unfortunate side effects like "weight gain" and "breast tissue enlargement," and in the case of estrogen therapy, "increased risk of heart disease or stroke." In time, he stopped listening altogether. The doctor went on for what seemed an abnormally long time, his voice receding into the background as though it were coming from far away, or being filtered through some dreamlike other reality where interaction was neither relevant nor possible, parallel to but not actually within Tom's reality.

He wants to cut off my balls, he was thinking, over and over again, trying to understand what that *meant,* what it *would mean,* and at the same time knowing exactly what it meant and would mean. He could hear Fran asking questions about pain and the difficulties of the various procedures and the possible side effects, thinking *I can't do it,* and he could hear the doctor offering explanations to her in a comforting tone—and to him too although he had withdrawn and wanted no further explanations. Then he heard the doctor circling back again to "bilateral orchiectomy" as being, in his view, "the surest and best of the hormonal therapy alternatives," and speaking reassuringly of how contrary to the many irrational fears men had, there were no voice changes that resulted from the procedure, and while the likelihood of impotence was admittedly almost one hundred per cent, an implant made during the procedure could keep a man's appearance as natural as if nothing had been done. *Appearance.*

"What are the odds?" he blurted out, interrupting with a question that he realized even as he uttered it was a non-sequitur to whatever the doctor was saying. He didn't care. It was the only thing that had significance in the face of all the gibberish he had been hearing. *Don't give me these fucking euphemisms,* he thought, *that make it sound like what you're doing is something positive*—therapy, *for Chrissakes!*

"I'm sorry, Tom. The odds to what?"

"This castration you're talking about. What are the odds? How long would I have?"

"Tom," Fran said, as though he had breached some unspoken protocol of medical etiquette. As though there was no room for plain, straightforward language in this discussion of his fate.

He ignored her and spoke again to the doctor, looking straight into his eyes. "I want to do whatever will buy me the most time, although I don't want it if it means something long and dragged out and expensive to my family."

Dr. Marshall's gaze was searching and steady. "Then I would advise you to have the surgery. It's the simplest and least expensive procedure, and the long-term survival rate is at least as good as the alternatives."

He looked at Dr. Marshall as though they were involved in a high-stakes poker game together and the doctor had just called his bluff. "I'll think about it," he said. "I need to think about it."

In the days that followed it was about the only thing he *could* think about. Nothing else seemed to matter. The Christmas season was fully upon them but he had no interest in it. Through all their years together he and Fran—and for many years Ben too—had maintained a tradition he loved of cutting their own Christmas tree and then trimming and decorating it on the first Sunday of December, but this year he had no desire to do any of it. Fran went out one day with Ben, Marie and Teddy to pick out a tree for each household, and Fran decorated theirs mostly by herself while he sat and looked on. She did her best to make the occasion as festive as it normally was, playing the Bing Crosby and Nat King Cole Christmas music he had always sung to and enjoyed and that Ben, as a teenager, had sneered at, and he *tried* to be involved, he really did, by helping her string the lights and by sometimes handing her ornaments that she almost invariably reminisced about, but his heart was not in it, he remained silent during most of the process, and when it came time for placing the star atop the tree, he declined her invitation to do it. It was, he understood, a profound moment, marking the first time this had ever happened. The star dated back to their first Christmas together as a couple, when they had little money for ornaments and decided to make their own. They strung popcorn and cranberries that year, and through a small outlay of money for craft materials—cloth and ribbons and styrofoam balls—they created all their own ornaments, a few of which they still used. It was the star though, cut from yellow felt and glued to a piece of cardboard, that had become, through the years, a symbol of something central to and more than Christmas. Exactly what it represented he did not know, but every year Ben as a young boy had pleaded to be the one to put the star up and he had always resisted, explaining to Ben that he was too small and it was too dangerous to climb up so high and lean over, but that when Ben was taller than he was, he would gladly let Ben do it. It was part joke—in the days of that father-son banter when Ben used to insist he would grow taller than his father—and part something else. That day had never come, of course, and by the time he understood that Ben would *never* be taller and offered him the job anyway, probably sometime early in Ben's teenage years, Ben scoffed at the idea and said, *"You* do it. It doesn't matter to me."

Now, with his back compromising him and the decision about what to do weighing him down, it did not matter to him either. He kept coming up against the notion that if he did what Dr. Marshall was suggesting, he would no longer be a man, at least not by any definition he had ever considered important. *No balls. He's got no balls.* It was what men said about any man who was somehow not measuring up, not being a man. *No cojones.* No courage. No guts. No strength or determination or daring. *No sexual prowess*—he would never make love again in his life to Fran, not in the way that he had always considered to be the truest way to make love to a woman. In recent months their lovemaking had not been what it used to be due to his urinary difficulties, nowhere near as frequent or, for him, as carefree, but they had still *had* a love life, and he had still, albeit self-consciously and not always reliably, been able to have an erection and intercourse and bring both Fran and himself to orgasm. If he had the operation—if he allowed himself to be *castrated*—none of this would be possible any longer, and worse still, he would probably not even care. He would lose not just the ability to engage in sexual intercourse, but also the *desire* to be a sexual being.

He had never been one of those gung-ho macho types who believed that all of what it meant to be a man revolved around a prick and a set of balls and a hard-ass attitude. Being a man meant more to him than simply being aggressive and forceful and stoic and tough, ready at any moment to slam down a whiskey or throw himself into a good fistfight. The types in American folklore and pop culture—the Daniel Boones and John Waynes and Humphrey Bogarts—had always seemed to him caricatures, and despite all the ribbing he had taken as a teenager about being the "Score King," he had never viewed sex as a kind of game where the object was to jump into bed with as many women as possible. Sex had never been for him the accumulation of points and the cataloguing of stories for the pleasure of swapping exaggerations and lies with a bunch of cronies. The fraternity mentality in American males disgusted him, had disgusted him since even before he went to college and saw altogether too much of it firsthand. It was in college that he had met Fran, and he had been faithful to her in thought, if not always in deed, ever since. For as long as he could recall he had believed that men could be sensitive and generous and loyal, and contrary to so much of what American males were exposed to and led to assume, not everything about being a man was tied to an erect penis and prolific sex. But the thought of having his testicles removed frightened him, in a way, more than the cancer itself, and he could neither get his mind around it long enough to accept it, nor get his mind away from it long enough to give it perspective. No matter how he turned the thought over, he could not escape the conclusion that even though having testicles should not and did not define *everything* about him as a man, it did define something *essential* about him as a man, something recognized by every culture throughout all of history, and to lose this essential element of his manhood would also mean losing something *essential* about who he was. He was, uniquely, Thomas A. Derringer, but Thomas A. Derringer was, and had always been, *a man*.

At first Fran tried to get him to talk about it, but he told her he needed time to think, so she said nothing more than that she would support whatever he wanted to do. She stayed home more often than usual to tend to his needs, cooked meals for him and remained solicitous about his pain, but she did not directly address the matter of what he should do until after several days had passed and she could no longer contain herself. His silences had seemed to her to be growing longer and deeper, and he himself more distant and self-absorbed. She feared that he was moving into a world of his own somewhere beyond her reach.

"Tom, I think it's time we talked about what to do," she said at last. "You've been so quiet lately I don't know what you're thinking."

She sat next to him on the couch in the living room where he was reading the newspaper, which he found gave him little pleasure anymore. Most of what he read struck him as irrelevant or insignificant. He put the paper down but did not reply right away and did not look at her, so she reached for his hand and held it in both of hers and waited patiently for him.

"I don't know what to tell you," he said, avoiding her gaze while looking off at nothing in particular. "I'm not even sure I *know* what I'm thinking."

She stroked his hand softly and waited for him to continue.

"There seems to be no good solution. That's about as far as I can get when I think about what to do. I've looked over the material Dr. Marshall gave us, as well as a lot of the information Ben printed out, and I keep coming to the conclusion that all the procedures are either too drastic or too expensive or have too many debilitating side effects. Or all of the above. And then I think, why bother with any of it?"

In the pause that followed the question he looked at her for the first time and felt a sudden pang of remorse. She was doing her best to listen and keep herself positive, but those dear blue eyes of hers could not mask her disappointment. "I realize how selfish that sounds, but I'm trying to be honest about this. I don't see anything that makes me say, 'This looks good. Let's do it.' The choices strike me as no choices at all. Hobson's choice."

She had also read over the information and understood the reason for his pessimism, but where he saw fifty per cent of all men dying before two years with his type of cancer, no matter the treatment involved, she saw fifty per cent surviving. And where he saw no choices, she saw clear ones, each with its own advantages and disadvantages, but choices nevertheless. It was the way they had always been as a couple—he viewed life through the lenses of skepticism and doubt, she through possibility and hope. Neither had always been right, of course, and it was the balance between them that had provided their enduring strength together.

"If you were to have the operation the doctor suggested, you wouldn't even have to stay in the hospital overnight."

"And I'd be a eunuch for life. A bloated, breasty eunuch."

"But you'd be alive, and it would greatly reduce your pain and increase your chances of living longer. Tom, I want you alive. I don't care about the rest of it."

"I *do*." He sat up straighter and withdrew his hand from hers. "See, that's the problem. I *do* care about the rest of it. I don't want to go through whatever time I have left in my life without being able to make love to you, and I don't want to look in the mirror and see myself becoming someone else. I don't want to *feel* like I'm someone else. I want to be who I am and who I've always been. Is that so unreasonable?"

She moved closer to him on the couch and took his hand again, fearful and determined. She could understand his objections completely—she knew Tom better than he knew himself, she sometimes thought. But this was a battle she did not want to lose, a battle not so much against him as *for* him. "Of course not. But do you think you're the same person now as before we had Ben? Or before we were married? I know I'm not. I'm a much different person now than I was when we first met in college. Sometimes I even think it's as though we live several lives in one lifetime. I think about who I was just ten years ago, and I'm not even sure about that. I was still working at the school and I wasn't even close to being a grandmother yet. Life changes us, Tom, and if we live long enough, it changes us many times."

Her words made impeccable sense to him, which was why he wanted to object so vehemently to them. There was no doubt that living his life with her all these years had changed him, unquestionably for the better (he hated to think of what he might be like had he not met her); or that having Ben as a son had brought him a kind of fulfillment he had never believed possible and could hardly put into words, especially to Ben, had humbled him and made him far less cynical, far more appreciative of life's potential for joy; or that the presence of his grandson had humbled him further still by showing him a new kind of love, more pure than anything he had known because there were no strings attached, no burdensome responsibilities or expectations on either side, and at the same time more powerful because it connected all of his past to the limitless future beyond him and thus transcended time. And yet he found himself resenting her for bringing these things up, these pillars of sense, as if somehow they could bear the enormous weight of what was senseless.

"You're right, but I guess I just don't like the idea that I have no real choice about how I change, or how much I change." He knew as soon as he said this that there was something self-pitying and not quite honest about it, though he did not try to follow the deception to its source.

"I don't want to minimize any of what you're feeling," she said earnestly, shaking her head. "Believe me, I don't want this change in our lives any more than you do." She paused, and her eyes began to well up and her voice grew shaky as she continued. "And I didn't mean to imply that anything about this is normal, or that we shouldn't try to retain some core of ourselves through all the changes in our lives." She sought to clear the tears from her eyes with her fingertips. "It's just that I love you very much, and I don't want you to avoid doing something that could save your life because of the way it would change you. It wouldn't change my feelings for you. Never."

She trembled and broke down after saying this, and he gathered her in to himself and stroked her hair. "I know," he said. "I know." He felt at once sorry for her as well as for himself, for the grim prospects of his life, and cheapened by a sense that he had played a sympathy card that had worked.

Chapter Nine

Better to Give

The decision to have the operation did not come without a good deal of second thoughts and retractions. One moment he would decide, he thought, with complete finality and conviction that he would go ahead with it, and ten minutes later he would find himself literally quivering at the prospect of what that finality meant, wanting to snap the decision back like a wayward dog on a leash. Even after he had told Fran of his decision and called Dr. Marshall to set up an appointment for the operation, he found himself waffling back and forth, although he never let on to Fran.

"I've decided to go ahead with the bilateral orchiectomy," he heard himself saying to Dr. Marshall, with Fran standing near him as he made the call. In the moment of saying it it struck him as absurd and unreal, as if he were hearing someone else speak, as if he were detached from his body and hearing someone else—one of his clients, perhaps—whose voice sounded just like his own, pronounce the fateful words as if he had finally decided that French doors would, after all, be the best choice for his study. "If we could schedule it as soon as possible, I'd appreciate that." "Of course," the doctor said, "I'll have my secretary work with you to set up a time." And then, "Tom, I know this is a difficult decision for you, but I think it's the right thing to do."

He thought so too or he would not have called, but immediately after the secretary helped him schedule the date and he got off the phone, he thought, *My God, what have I done?* He ran through his list of reasons as if it were a litany of prayers to comfort him: he wanted to live, and *without pain;* he wanted to act rather than be passive; he wanted to follow the simplest course—no complicated and expensive injections for the rest of his life; and above all else, he wanted to do what was least disruptive and least expensive to his family—*he did not want his life to be a burden to others.* But his thoughts kept circling back to the same two inevitable questions: *Can my life really have come to this? Can this really be happening to me?*

"Are you all right, Tom?" Fran asked him after he had placed the phone back in its cradle. "You're still sure about this?"

He nodded, and she came forward and hugged him.

Can my life really have come to this? Can this really be happening to me? It seemed impossible. It seemed as though the last thirty years—no, more than that, the last *forty*—had gone by in a heartbeat. A duality of sorts seemed to be present, or a kind of fundamental contradiction between perception and reality. He had been aware of its existence for many years, but never so acutely as now. He felt as young and vital and alive as he had when he was twenty, and yet he was not twenty, he was sixty. And he remembered the feeling, the belief, the certainty he had possessed as a young man—as clearly as if it were still present and true in his life—that although his own death was an inevitable truth, he would not be learning that truth for quite a long time. The syllogism he had first heard in a philosophy class—*Caius is a man. All men are mortal. Therefore, Caius is mortal.*—proved only that he, along with everyone else who lived, would one day die, but it did not prove when. Other people died every day, sometimes people very near and dear, but he himself had too much living left to do to be overly concerned with dying. Dying was for other people, not for him. Not yet. Still, here was this pain in his bones that he could not deny, and here was this operation that must be performed, and here was this sense of seriousness and trepidation about his condition that everyone around him seemed to accept as justified.

"We were able to schedule it before Christmas," he said matter-of-factly, and after a moment added, "Merry Christmas."

"If it could only just take your pain away..." Fran said, and did not finish the thought.

No, it would not be a gift. Never. Not when you paid so much for it. "It's amazing that an operation so simple can have such dramatic consequences. Zip, zip, zip—sort of like Zorro—and they're done, and you're never the same afterwards."

"But if it stops the cancer from spreading..."

"I know, I know. That's the tradeoff. That's the deal. Only it seems like a deal with the devil."

"I can't look at it that way," Fran said with conviction. "To me, this operation means you're giving yourself a chance. You're giving *us*—*all* of us—a chance. And I am very, very grateful for that." She looked up at him and gently stroked the side of his face with her fingertips. "Tom, sweetheart, I *know* this is not easy for you, but I don't know what I would do without you. Thank you for doing this."

He ran his fingers through Fran's silky gray hair and pressed her head gently to his chest, thinking of her and Ben and Marie and his grandson and his new grandchild to come. "I guess a deal of any kind is better than no deal at all," he said, trying to register a voice of quiet confidence. But when he thought again of the operation he was filled once more with doubt, and he worried that she could hear it, pressed up as she was against the rapid beating of his heart.

*   *   *

Fran had offered Ben and Marie a chance to do some Christmas shopping without Teddy, so a few days before the operation she took her grandson off their hands for the day. She planned to do a little shopping herself and promised Teddy that when they were finished she would buy him an ice cream. Tom felt well enough to join them. He had been taking his most recent medication around the clock for a couple of weeks now, and except for occasional instances of what Dr. Marshall termed "breakthrough pain"—sudden, sharp, unpredictable episodes for which he had a separate medication in the form of a lollipop-like lozenge—he had gained enough distance from his pain that he wanted to take advantage of every opportunity to get out of the house, especially if it meant spending time with his grandson. He brought the lozenge with him just in case though.

Together he and Fran fussed over getting Teddy properly into his car seat and laughed at how inept they were at doing so.

"You'd think I could get it right the first time just once," Fran said.

"Well, hey, it's not like we've had a lot of practice at this, you know. Don't be so hard on yourself."

"I just hate to feel so...so *clumsy.*"

"Grammy, what's clumsy?" Teddy asked. Tom smiled at the earnest expression on his grandson's face, realizing it was this perhaps more than anything else that he enjoyed in children so young—their ability to ask simple questions with no hint of guile.

"Clumsy," she repeated as she fumbled with the straps and latches for a moment more and then gave up in mock disgust and said to Tom, "Here, you do it." She looked at Teddy and frowned and pursed her lips. "Clumsy is...what would you say clumsy is, Grampa?"

Tom stopped trying to fasten the car seat buckle and looked at his grandson with exaggerated thoughtfulness. "Clumsy is not being able to do something very well that you think you should be able to do, like walking." Tom took a few steps away from the car in a normal walk, but on his return swayed with each step as if he were wildly drunk. Teddy laughed and said, "Grammy, Grampa's *clumsy!*"

"Yes, he is. And silly."

"Now let's get you into this car seat," Tom said. He found part of the problem was the bulky overcoat Teddy was wearing, and since the weather was fairly mild and they had been warming up the car for several minutes, he helped his grandson out of the coat. Then he centered the straps over Teddy's shoulders and latched the car seat with ease. "That's a very nice sweater you have on," he said of the royal blue vest with red and white sailboats that Fran had knitted for her grandson. "I wish I had one like it."

"When it grows up maybe you can wear it, Grampa."

"That's very nice of you, Teddy. Thank you." He looked to Fran and they smiled at each other. *A child's reality,* he thought, and understood with a sudden sensation of loss how many years he had been without that reality in his life, and how much he had missed it. He remembered how Ben as a two year old had once looked at a block of cheese with a knife stuck in the middle at an acute angle and had said, "Wook, a sailboat!" It had taken him a moment to understand what Ben was referring to since they were at home and there was no body of water and no boat visible through any window. "I see," he had said at last, after moving next to Ben and following his gaze. He had wondered then as he did now with his grandson at what point such a fresh view of the world began to disappear. *Why* did it disappear? By what mechanism was it replaced? And once it was gone, was it gone forever, or did it merely lay dormant, waiting to be discovered again as an adult—could an adult learn to see and feel again what children saw and felt? Or were the two mutually exclusive, an adult by definition viewing the world with less imagination and sensitivity—as a more concrete and immutable place—than did a child?

He remembered another time when Ben was not quite four and the two of them watched an animated version of *CHARLOTTE'S WEB*. Fran was out somewhere that evening and they were curled up together on the couch—they did that quite often when Ben was very young. Near the end, when Charlotte died, he could feel Ben trembling and there were tears welling up in his eyes, but Ben did not say anything. It was not until a few moments later when Wilbur was trying to find names for the runts of Charlotte's brood that Ben broke down into great sorrowful sobs and said, "Why did she die?" He did his best to explain, but Ben continued sobbing for some time, and when he asked Ben why he was so upset Ben disarmed him completely. "They won't know their mother," Ben whimpered, and he understood then that Ben was crying not just for Charlotte and her orphaned children but for himself, for his incipient understanding of death and loss, for the possibility that his own mother might die also and he would no longer know her. It was the human condition that his not quite four year old son cried for, and as a father he was left dumbstruck. There *was* nothing he could say, and so he merely held Ben in his arms for a long time afterwards, rocking gently back and forth, his own heart swollen with pride and grief, until his son fell asleep.

What happened to that *child's reality* over the course of a lifetime? Was it too painful to maintain? Was that it? Did we leave it behind because it was too heavy a weight, too difficult a burden to carry with us throughout our lives? He recalled a line he had read or heard that the only people who understood what life meant, and then only somewhat—for moments, maybe—were saints and poets, but he wondered if children should not also be included, because surely they saw and felt more about life than most adults did.

A Salvation Army worker was ringing a bell in front of one of the downtown stores as they strolled along. They liked to shop downtown as often as possible because this was *their town*, they knew people here, had friends who owned or worked for some of the businesses, and they disliked the notion of supporting the corporate anonymity of the malls that had put some of their friends out of business and laid waste to the whole concept of a downtown community. This time of year, though, with all the lights and festive decorations and unique shops, he was sure the downtown businesses must do reasonably well.

"Who is that, Grampa?" Teddy asked, pointing from his perch in the stroller to the matronly woman ringing the bell. She wore a hat and glasses and the standard navy blue uniform, and she nodded and smiled at passersby who dropped money into her kettle.

"That's someone who likes to help people who are less fortunate than we are," he said, and felt the inadequacy of such an explanation. "Not everybody has enough food to eat or clothes like your nice sweater to keep them warm."

"Oh," was all his grandson said.

"Do you think you could put this into the lady's big red kettle for me, Teddy?" he asked, folding a five dollar bill in half and then in half again before handing it to Teddy.

"Yes," Teddy said, although he needed to be lifted up out of the stroller to reach the opening. The woman smiled and nodded at the two of them and continued ringing the bell but did not speak as Teddy dropped the money into the kettle.

"She didn't say 'thank you,'" Teddy blurted out as they moved away.

"That's okay, sweetheart," Fran said. "She said 'thank you' with her eyes."

"Mommy says you should always say 'thank you.'"

"Well, Mommy's right. When someone gives us something we should always say 'thank you.' But sometimes people say 'thank you' in other ways than with their voices, and sometimes, even, people *have* to say 'thank you' without their voices." Fran bent low so that she could speak to Teddy at his eye level in the stroller. "Do you like to leave cookies and carrots out for Santa and his reindeer when they come at Christmas?"

Teddy nodded.

"I do too. Well, that's a way of saying 'thank you' to Santa and Rudolph and all the other reindeer for coming to give us presents when we can't use our voices to say it to them. Do you understand?"

Teddy nodded again.

"Did Mommy and Daddy also teach you about giving to other people?"

Teddy shook his head.

"Christmas is a time of year when lots of people give presents to each other. You know that, right?" He nodded. "You'll be getting lots of presents from people too, and it's easy to think getting presents is what Christmas is all about; but I want you to try to remember something that's very hard for most people to remember: *It's better to give than to receive.* Do you think you can remember that?"

"It's better to give than to receive," Teddy repeated dutifully.

"That's *very* good. You're such a smart boy!" she said, her face beaming close to his. "But do you know what that means, Teddy?"

He shook his head again.

"Think about Santa. He gives to everybody, doesn't he, and he's a *very* happy man. He's always smiling! And when you and Grampa put that money into the big red kettle, you were giving something to somebody else. That's a *very* good thing to do. That money might help to buy a nice pair of shoes or a shirt for a little boy or girl who doesn't have any nice clothes. Don't you think that's a good thing to do?"

Teddy nodded, as he knew he was supposed to do.

"I know it's a hard thing for a little boy to understand, but it's important to try. You can do that for me, can't you?"

"Yes, Grammy."

"I knew you could. Thank you, sweetie." She patted him on his lap and stood up again.

"And one other thing, Teddy." This time it was Grampa speaking as they walked along, and Teddy felt himself growing tired and wondered if they would ever get to the place where they were going to have ice cream. Something told him though that now would not be a good time to ask. "It's not just at Christmas that it's better to give to other people. It's the whole year. It's every day. That's a pretty tall order, isn't it?"

He knew that he should nod his head once again, and then he waited for what seemed like a very long time to see if they wanted to say anything more. When they did not, at last he said, "Are we almost at the ice cream place?"

He was not sure what was funny, but both his grandparents laughed, and Grammy said, "Of course, sweetheart. You've been very patient."

At the ice cream parlor they took a booth across from a woman seated alone that Tom thought he recognized. She had wavy orange-red hair that was streaked heavily with gray and looked dry and brittle, and she was picking absently at the remains of a dinner. Her cheeks, like the rest of her body, were puffy and bloated, and her hazel eyes had fleshy bags beneath them. If it was indeed who he thought, she must be at least sixty pounds heavier than the slender young carrot top he remembered having dated two or three times in high school, in the days when he was one of the most sought-after boys in the entire school.

"Jenny?" he said.

She turned to look at him. "Yes," she said, her voice low and incurious. It was clear she did not know who he was.

"It's Tom, Tom Derringer. From way back in high school." Her eyes brightened slightly with the light of recognition. "How are you, Jenny? We probably haven't seen each other in what, forty years?"

"Must be at least that," she said, her tone suggesting she had no desire to go back there. "I'm all right."

It was turning out to be one of those awkward moments for all that made him regret having started up the conversation. Better to have kept quiet and pretended not to know her.

"Jenny, this is my wife, Fran, and my grandson, Teddy."

Fran said "hello" and prodded Teddy to do the same. Jenny nodded and turned again toward her dinner. Fran went back to helping Teddy with the coloring he had started using the crayons and placemat provided by the restaurant. Tom had an uncomfortable feeling of having pushed an advantage over Jenny, as if—unintentional though it may have been—he had flaunted a condition of greater prosperity.

"You married Eric Belanger, didn't you, Jenny?" He remembered the always smiling, wisecracking kid he had gone skiing with once or twice in high school and wanted to give something to her, share with her, at least, the fondness he felt for Eric.

She looked at him. "Eric died of cancer almost a year ago to the day."

"I'm sorry," he said, and felt immediately chastened. He wanted to say to her that he too had cancer, and that he was due shortly to undergo an operation he dreaded because the cancer had spread to his bones, but since he was still alive this too seemed only a kind of one-upmanship and he kept it to himself. "I'm very sorry. Eric was a great guy."

Fran looked over to offer condolences also, but Jenny was no longer looking their way and seemed to be gathering herself to leave.

Tom rose abruptly from the booth and said, "Teddy, do you need to go to the bathroom?" Teddy shook his head. "I'll be right back." The urge to piss had been mounting terribly in him for the past ten minutes, and he was afraid he might begin to wet himself at any moment if he didn't leave right away.

When he returned, he could see that Jenny was gone and the ice cream had been served to them. But before he could reach their booth the onset of a sudden, sharp pain in his back, at once familiar and surprising, buckled his knees and hobbled him. Teddy, who already had a thick ring of vanilla circumscribing his lips, chuckled and said, "Grammy, Grampa's being clumsy again!"

Fran turned around, saw what was happening, and moved immediately to his side. "Tom, are you all right?"

"I'm okay, I'm okay," he managed as she helped him to his seat. "Just need a lozenge, is all." He found what he was looking for in his pocket, used his pocket knife to help him cut through the heavy foil wrapper, and placed the lozenge between his cheek and gum like a lollipop. He closed his eyes and tasted the raspberry flavor and waited a few excruciating moments until the effects began to kick in. It was amazing, really, that such intense pain could be lessened so quickly. He opened his eyes and saw that both Fran and Teddy were looking at him, Teddy's look of concern giving way almost instantly to a beaming smile. "Grampa, can I have a lollipop too?"

The thought of it sent a tremor along his spine and caused him to make a mental note to be sure, when he got home, that none of his medications—but especially this one—could be discovered by his grandson. This one, so alluringly like a sweet-tasting lollipop, could kill him. This one he would have to hide well.

"Teddy, this isn't a real lollipop. It's called a lozenge, and it's a special kind of medicine that only Grampa can take, okay? It's to make me feel better. But I don't want you to ever, ever, ever try it, okay, because it wouldn't make *you* feel better. It would make *you* very sick."

"Other lollipops are all right for you, Teddy, but not this kind," Fran said. "How's the ice cream?"

"Good." He licked his lips and said, "Grampa, sometime you can have one of my lollipops if you need to feel better."

"Thank you, Teddy. That's very generous of you." He closed his eyes again. The lozenge was beginning to take effect more fully now, relaxing him and pushing the pain to a more remote outpost of his consciousness. Instead of the pain he found himself thinking about his grandson's offer, which made him smile and prompted the sudden realization that going ahead with the operation *was* the right thing to do. It was the most meaningful thing he could give his family, when he got right down to it. He had always said he would do anything, *give* anything for his family. Now he was about to have that belief tested. That's all it was, really, another test, this time a test of his devotion to his family.

He opened his eyes again at the sound of Fran whispering something to Teddy that ended in "remember?" and Teddy nodding his head vigorously, saying, "Yeah, yeah."

"Grampa, that lady said to tell you 'thank you.'"

"Did she ask *you* to tell me?"

Teddy nodded.

"Well, thank you for remembering."

"What did you do, Tom, pay for her meal?"

He nodded his head. "She seemed very sad and very lonely."

"Yes, she did."

And Eric *was* a great guy. He had meant that with all his heart.

The operation went as smoothly as anyone could have hoped. *Too* smoothly, in a way. The ease with which he could enter the hospital a whole man, *a man,* and return home from it on the same day *less* than whole was truly unnerving. The operation was such a simple one, relatively speaking, that it required only a local anesthetic and a single small incision that allowed both testicles to be removed and the implant to be made (appearances *did* have their value, he had decided—he could not quite abide the idea of feeling an empty sac), after which he was stitched up and released from the hospital without even having to stay overnight. The discomfort he felt over the next few days was minor compared to the bone pain he had been dealing with for so long now. Taken altogether, the simplicity of the procedure and its negligible physical pain afterward seemed completely disproportionate to the psychological and symbolic impact of it. It seemed to him that it *should* have been more painful and more physically traumatic, that somehow there should have been more suffering involved. At least then he could have said he had taken it all like a man, he had been forced to endure, to grit his teeth and bear up. Instead, it all seemed a sort of medical deception. A warped joke. Now you have balls, now you don't. Except that the absence was *permanent,* the loss irreversible, and no matter how he tried to rationalize it away ("There is nothing either good or bad, but thinking makes it so," a line whose origin he could not recall, kept coming to him from somewhere way back in his past), the reality of his new situation never left him for long. After each time he took a piss he would cup himself in his hand and look down and think about how useless this part of him had become, and it caused him such sorrow that he thought he would probably go mad if not for the thought he had done it for his family. He knew that he had done it for himself as well—he wanted to live, and without pain—but the greater incentive had been to not disappoint his family by refusing to fight, by dying without a battle, while at the same time not becoming a dependent burden to them and not depriving them of money they would need for the future. For it rightly to be a gift the burden *should* be his, not theirs, and if the only way to shoulder it was to suffer it inside himself, in the silent, private anguish of feeling less than a man, then so be it. It was in this interior life, away from the public eye, where all the real battles in life took place anyway, where life was truly lived, where we were all most alone, most joyful, most terrified, and where no one could really follow, not even, perhaps, those who loved us best. Difficult as it might be, he would simply have to content himself with understanding and accepting these truths.

By Christmas he was no longer experiencing any breakthrough pain at all. He was continuing with his regular pain medication, although at a lower dosage, and he had started taking a drug to eliminate what Dr. Marshall explained were the five to ten per cent of the androgens remaining in his system even after the surgery. This drug he would have to take for the rest of his life. It had already begun to cause him occasional bouts of diarrhea that made him feel like he had little control of his body; and the noticeable swelling of breast tissue along with weight gain around his midsection, which he had always taken pride in keeping trim, increased his sense that by degrees his life was becoming less and less his own. But as promised he no longer experienced the kind of consistent pain that had diminished his capacity to enjoy life, and he no longer had to use the lozenges for breakthrough pain. For these changes, at least, he was thankful.

He and Fran spent Christmas Eve and the first part of Christmas morning at Ben's, where they all opened gifts and Teddy, the first and only grandchild (so far!), the first and only child of his first and only child, received the mother lode of presents. Tom took great pleasure in watching his grandson's approach to it all because it showed a level of maturity and appreciation that surprised him and made him think that perhaps adults should take lessons about Christmas from children, not the reverse. Teddy would open whatever gift was given to him and want to immerse himself in it immediately. If it was a book, he wanted someone to read it to him then and there. If it was a toy, such as the fire truck from him and Fran, Teddy wanted to begin playing with it right away, and would show no interest in opening another gift. In previous years Teddy was too young to have a clear idea of what Christmas involved, and the giving, receiving and opening of gifts, culminating in the bounty left by Santa on Christmas morning, was not yet predictable enough for him to develop any expectations. This year he was old enough to comprehend the exchange of gifts and the impending arrival of Santa, yet he still wanted nothing more than to spend time on whatever gift he had before him.

Tom had never realized until this Christmas how thoroughly the desire for something more was *taught* to kids by the very people who expected the opposite behavior. "Be happy with what you have" or "Be thankful for what you get" adults preached to kids throughout the year, ratcheting up the tone and frequency of such admonitions around the Christmas season, but when the big day came, when the time for practicing restraint and teaching gratitude reached its most important moments of truth, adults kept thrusting gifts under the noses of kids and demanding *dissatisfaction:* put that one aside so that you can *open this one!* And as soon as *this one* was opened, the requisite injunction followed, "What do you say?" followed by the requisite response, "Thank you!" As if the behavior of wanting to read the book or play with the toy was not the point at all, not when there were more gifts to be opened and a protocol that must be followed. *Don't be happy with what you have when there is more.* That was the real message. Was it any wonder that kids inevitably rebelled against adults? And all through the years he had been as guilty as everyone else of indoctrinating them with the message, of maintaining the hypocrisy, and just as oblivious that he had been doing it. This year, for whatever reason, he saw it all very clearly, as clearly as if he were watching a play from a front row seat, except that he was still one of the actors on stage himself.

"Teddy, you look like you're getting kind of tired," he said at one point on Christmas Eve when he thought his grandson might need a break. "Would you like to read that new book?" It was a book called *THE GIVING TREE* by Shel Silverstein that Fran had picked out. Teddy nodded. "Would that be okay?" he asked, turning to Ben and Marie.

"That would be nice," Marie said. "I'm sure he *is* getting tired."

"Afterwards it's bedtime, buddy," Ben said. "We'll read you *THE NIGHT BEFORE CHRISTMAS* and then you have to go to sleep so that Santa can come. You know he won't come if you're still awake, right?"

"I know."

Ben turned to his father and said, "Thanks, Dad."

"It's my pleasure." Which was the absolute truth. At the moment, there was nothing in all the world that he would rather do than curl his grandson into his lap and read a book to him.

After Christmas Tom decided he was not going to waste his time any longer on activities—or people—that he did not enjoy. During every moment of every day he wanted to be doing something positive, something that gave him pleasure and made him feel, at the end of the day, that it had been a good day, a day worth remembering. For all the talk about how short life was, most people managed to fill their days with things they would rather not be doing, and if they did that year after year without regard to the passing of time, it was likely that when the end came—if it came in such a way that they could even reflect long enough to pose a question—they would find themselves asking what it had all been for. What had they spent their lives—*their time*—doing, and why?

He was well aware of history's countless lessons that the chains of economic necessity and social position could severely limit choice. Those who through no fault of their own were born into slavery or abject poverty and forced to scrape away at mind-numbing work simply to exist, or those born female in cultures that saw fit to mutilate women's bodies and close off even their most basic freedoms—these people, with little or no opportunity to change their circumstances, might also ask at the end of their lives what it had all been for. But even when such conditions were not part of the equation, when people lived in generally prosperous circumstances that afforded a much greater opportunity for choice and a much wider range of possibilities, they filled their lives with minutiae, they found ways to waste it away. If you could, he thought, why not listen to Ode to Joy while washing dishes or cleaning the toilet? Why not pause for a few moments to look at the sky while shoveling snow or mowing the lawn? Why not try to *reduce* the number of tasks to be accomplished in a day rather than pack more of them into every hour, so that when evening came and you looked back upon what you had done, you could do more than tick off a laundry list of banal activities? Wasn't it better to be able to say, simply, "I read a good book today that made me think about my life" rather than to boast about how many hours you had worked or how much money you had made? Wasn't it more important to see the slanting rays of early morning sunlight glistening off the snow, or to have a conversation with an old friend you bumped into at the grocery store rather than to be so preoccupied with what you *should* be doing that you hurried through the present without ever being in it?

The more he thought about it, the more he realized that most people had it all wrong. *He* had had it all wrong during much of his life. In the pursuit of...what? some warped dream of material prosperity? the ingrained and never-ending habits of acquisition and accumulation?...he had spent a good deal of his life in a hurry to be somewhere else or to get something else. Like a junkie addicted to heroin he had been addicted to the chase of dreams that were not his own. He—the architect—had constructed his life on the soft footings of everything false and impermanent, and in the process had missed out on what was most important. Was it any wonder why he felt guilt about Ben whenever he thought about their inability to speak to each other? True, he had been there at Ben's birth and had taken time off to help Fran recuperate afterwards, and he had spent an occasional day skiing with his son when Ben was young, but when he thought honestly about it now he understood there had been too many times over the years when he had not been available for the little things in Ben's life. At three or four years old Ben used to wait for him by the window every day to see his car pull into the driveway, signifying his return from work, and he used to race out onto the porch and shout, "Daddy's home! Daddy's home!" jumping up and down all the while and shaking with excitement, face red and beaming with joy, his whole being utterly consumed by the moment as he waited for his father to draw near enough for him to leap finally into his arms and be swung around in that delirious delight of all children whose love cannot be contained, the two of them swinging around and around and Ben's joy spreading to him and making everything, *everything*, right with the world for that moment, and him saying, "How's my boy? How's my sweet boy?" But over time something had gone wrong. There had been too many opportunities lost—baseball games missed, school functions not attended. Had he even been to his son's high school graduation? He must have, but he could not remember it, probably had had his mind on other things and so had been present but had missed it all, and now those times were gone— *into the the past. The unremembered past, where too much of his life had gone.*

"Do you ever get the feeling," he said one evening to Fran when they were both reading quietly in the living room, "that we spend our lives searching for something that we're never quite able to find?"

"What do you mean?"

"I'm not sure. I'm not sure how to explain it. I guess it's a sense I get sometimes that we're all scurrying around looking for something, although it's not necessarily a conscious kind of looking and it's not at all clear what we're looking for. Suppose, for example, I were to stop people hustling from one place to another on the street or working diligently at their jobs or even shopping in a mall and ask them a simple question, 'What are you doing?' Most of them would probably give me a simple answer. 'Going to the bank,' or 'Working,' or 'Shopping' they would say. But if I were to take it a step further and ask, 'No, I mean, what are you doing in your life? What is it that pulls everything you do together? What is the glue that fastens this errand or this work or this shopping to the rest of your life? What connects one day to one week and one week to one year and one year to a lifetime? What is it that might be called the sort of overarching force that guides all of what you do?' Then what would they say? Maybe they'd say, 'I have no idea what you're talking about, buddy. Get lost!' I don't know. I guess I'm really not sure what they would say, but I think *I* would say I'm looking for something. I think we're *all* looking for something. We're all searching. That's what forms all the connections, so far as I can see. We're all searching from the moment we're born until the moment we die. For what, I don't know. Answers? Meaning? Love? Some way to fit in? I don't really know. It may be somewhat different from one person to the next. But I do think when you scrape everything away, at bottom we're all constantly searching."

"Now I see what you mean," Fran said, looking up from her book. "It's an interesting thought. But don't you think most people—whether they could put it into words this way or not—would say they're just trying to get by? Just trying to survive? If they're looking for anything, it's just a way to keep living from one day to the next, maybe with a little bit of happiness mixed in along the way."

"Well, yes, I think you're right. But amoebas are just trying to survive. People might say that and it might be true, but it doesn't mean that's *all* they're looking for from life. What you said about happiness, though, now that leads to something closer to the truth, I think."

"How do you mean?"

"I mean it's not enough for us to have only bread and water and shelter from one day to the next. We're looking for more than that from life. You know that as well as I do. Exactly what we're looking for I can't say, but happiness is a word that points us in the right direction. Maybe that's even *all* of what we're looking for, but we just don't know what happiness means or where to find it except in rare moments."

She looked at him and smiled, a hint of mischievousness creeping into her expression. "Some people might say it's God you're looking for, and you just haven't found Him yet."

"Maybe," Tom said without rising to the bait. The matters of God and religion had always been a source of friction between them, Fran having continued to be a faithful Catholic through the years while he had veered far away from faith, particularly any organized form of it, a long time ago. "But they could say that and still not know what God means," he said, his voice at once solemn and passionate. "The point is, I don't care what it's called. I don't care whether it's called God or heaven or happiness or nirvana or moksha. The word doesn't matter. It's the notion that we're searching for something we can't seem to find that concerns me."

He had been looking directly at her as he said this but he stopped now and looked away thoughtfully, then took a deep breath and exhaled. "Maybe what I'm talking about is the perfect life. Maybe that's what I'm trying to say and why I'm having so much trouble saying it. But I mean, imagine for a moment that somehow you had the power to create a perfect life for yourself. What would that be? Could you even begin to imagine it?" He was gazing at her again now, with something almost imploring in his eyes.

Fran held his gaze for a moment before she looked down and said, hesitantly, with a kind of shyness in her voice, "I'm living it."

"You don't have to say that. I wasn't asking for that from you."

"I know you weren't, but I mean it. Oh, there might be a few things I would change, if I could. I'd change all the killing in the world today, and the poverty. I'd start with those things, definitely. But if it's just in my own life you're talking about, apart from maybe redoing the kitchen cabinets or finding a nice painting for that space on the living room wall I've been wanting to decorate for twenty years, there's nothing I would change. I have you, and I have my health, and I have Ben and Marie and Teddy and a new baby on the way—really, to be able to do the things I love to do, with those I love the most, what more could I possibly ask for from life? Except, of course, for *your* health."

The shyness in her voice gave way to earnestness as she peered into his eyes and said, "Now let me ask you something. Why? Why is all of this bothering you so much?"

"I don't know. Maybe it's because of the cancer. Maybe it's because I don't have testosterone to distract me anymore." (She noticed he was not smiling when he said this. There was no hint of irony or sarcasm in his voice.) "It's strange, because on the one hand I feel less tension than I ever have in my life before— and everything seems magnified to me, or clearer somehow, more lucid. But on the other hand I feel a kind of urgency I've also never felt before. It's difficult to explain, except to say that the paradoxes seem greater. Little things seem both smaller and more significant. Big things seem less significant and yet even more important to understand."

They were both quiet for a moment as they pondered his words. "I guess I just don't want to see you getting yourself too worked up," she said.

"I'm okay. Really. It's not a *bad* state to be in. It's a *good* one. I only wish I'd been able to see things this way every day of my life. It puts a premium on not wasting time, and sometimes I feel like I've done far too much of that over the years. You know, that I could have done more, given more." *Especially to Ben,* he thought.

"I think everyone feels that way at times, Tom. It's impossible to feel like you've done everything right, everything the way you'd want, all the time. It's not human. We all make mistakes, we all wish we could take back something we said or did and say it or do it differently. But we can't. We're human beings. We're *not* perfect. We *make* mistakes. We *waste* time." She looked at him with mock consternation. "So quit expecting yourself to be something you can't. If you were a saint, I don't think I could live with you."

He smiled. "If I were a saint, I don't think I could live with myself. But I don't think we need to worry about that anytime soon." He could see by the expression on her face that the levity was reassuring to her, as it was to him also, but it did not diminish the confusion in his heart or the sense of urgency that accompanied him every hour of the day like the internal ticking of a clock.

It was during this time that he began thinking of how much he would like to give something to Ben.. At first he knew only that he wanted to give something that would last, something that would endure and have meaning to both of them, but the specific nature of it eluded him. Everything he thought of seemed superficial or flawed, sometimes both. A large sum of money? Helpful maybe, but far too impersonal—almost obscene, really. A new car? Pragmatic in some respects, but again, impersonal at best, and at worst an example of the kind of material consumerism that Ben so often railed against. A first-edition copy of one of Ben's favorite authors, Mark Twain perhaps? Nice thought, but probably very expensive and not something Tom himself particularly shared with Ben. Finally, out of mounting desperation, he confided his wish to Fran, who promptly got him on the right track.

"What about something related to fishing?" she asked, and he knew immediately what it was that he would like to give to Ben: a bamboo fly rod similar to his own, preferably one that he could put together himself. As soon as he thought of it he knew it was perfect; he had cherished his own rod as much as anything in life short of the people he loved most dearly.

"You're a gem, you know that?" he said, and kissed her on the forehead. "Truly a gem!"

So with a sense of joy and purpose in his heart he set about searching for how he might find a kit that would allow him to build the rod, or at least some of it, himself. His first thought was to take a trip to the Kittery Trading Post, probably his favorite store on earth. With its emphasis on gear and clothing for the outdoors, he thought of it as a sort of modest version of L.L Bean, another store he had always enjoyed, but the appeal of the Trading Post was that it was local and, to his mind, a good deal less pretentious. Bean was still worth the trip up north once in a while, but its phenomenal growth over the past thirty years and its marketing to the yuppy crowd had created a product line a bit too trendy and high-priced for him. During his last time in the store a Bean-employed fly fisherman with impeccably close-cropped silver hair and accoutered in fashionable fishing vest and waders had slipped into the sparkling clear pool in the center of the store, where he used a microphone headset to narrate to the gathered crowd as he cast a small fly rod for the outsized brook trout swimming about the pool. When the fish did not immediately rise to his fly, he kept chumming for them with fish food until he could hook one on the line and continue with his routine. Hardly the stuff of Izaak Walton, and surely not something you'd find at the Trading Post, where time spent browsing in the store itself or talking with one of the knowledgeable staff was never time wasted. But the Trading Post did not have anything like what he was looking for, although the person he spoke with gave him some good leads, one of which was to try Orvis, another legendary outdoor outfitter. He telephoned Orvis and discovered there was no such thing as a bamboo rod-building "kit," and to build a bamboo rod from scratch was hardly possible for the average person because there was too much equipment involved. Working with cane was such a trial and error process that typically a builder would buy the materials to build at least thirty rods in the hope that twenty of them would turn out to be passable. Building only one rod was too risky—you might put a good deal of time and energy into it only to find that it was no good. This was certainly not what he wanted to hear—he had neither the time nor the energy for such risk—but he did learn that a company called Angler's Workshop in the state of Washington sold "blanks," which were relatively finished pieces of bamboo that could be purchased along with reel seats and cork handles and all the other components so that in effect you *could* essentially custom build your own bamboo rod. He grew excited when he learned this and thanked the sales person from Orvis, "It's exactly what I'm looking for."

But when he telephoned Angler's Workshop he was discouraged to find they had sold their entire inventory of bamboo rod blanks to an individual in California who apparently had intentions of building and selling the rods himself. "When do you expect to get more blanks in?" he asked the pleasant young woman who had been answering all his questions.

"I'm not sure we'll ever get any more in," she said. "There's not much demand for them. They're so expensive they don't sell very quickly."

"Just out of curiosity, how much were you selling them for when you had them?"

"Oh, I think we sold them for about two hundred and ninety dollars."

Small price to pay for an heirloom, he thought. "Thank you very much," he said, and hung up the phone feeling defeated even in this seemingly modest and simple undertaking. It did not seem like too much to ask—to build a bamboo rod that he could give to his son, something that Ben could carry with him for a lifetime. But maybe it was. Maybe he was only trying to build something of himself to give to Ben. *Maybe it's nothing but an example of my own conceit,* he fretted, and began to think that perhaps his being thwarted was as it should be.

Then another thought abruptly came to him and chilled him to the core: *Give him your own rod.* In the very moment he thought it he knew it was what he must do. He must clean and polish the rod and give it to his son, and he knew too that Ben would not want to accept it while he was still alive. *Still alive.* That was the heart of the matter. To give it to Ben while he was still alive meant that he no longer expected to use it. And what did it mean that he no longer expected to use it? *What did it mean?*

Not long after the operation another PSA test showed his PSA level had dropped to near zero, which Dr. Marshall said he had hoped for and expected. It was a good indicator that Tom's cancer was being contained. But several weeks later, sometime in March, the level had risen dramatically, which coincided with renewed episodes of breakthrough pain that sent Tom back to using the lozenges he had hidden away in his dresser. This was *not* what the doctor had expected, and Tom could read from his eyes what his words would never come right out and say: *We gave it our best shot and it didn't work. Now, I'm afraid, you're a dead man.*

"Tom, Fran, I don't want to mislead you at all. This development is obviously not what we had hoped for. The cancer is proving to be even more aggressive than we had anticipated, which means we'll have to be more aggressive in our treatment of it."

More aggressive than cutting off my balls? he wanted to argue, feeling a mixture of contempt and absurdity wash through him. He knew that Dr. Marshall was not the enemy; he was merely the obligatory, if reluctant, messenger, and a sympathetic one at that, but still he could not speak.

"What does that mean, being 'more aggressive'?" Fran asked on his behalf as she looked from him to the doctor. She could feel her insides churning, her heart beating so hard it was all she could do to speak, but she wanted the doctor's words, wanted him to keep talking, as if somehow in continuing he would eventually be forced to concede that things were not as bad as he had just made them sound, not as bad as she felt, with a shudder, in her soul.

"It means we'll have to begin treating it with radiation," Dr. Marshall said to her, and then looked at Tom with a patient, benign expression. "The radiation will slow the cancer's spread and ease your pain. And we may want to consider trying some chemotherapy as well." The doctor must have read something in his look that gave away the quiver he felt in the pit of his stomach—he was no longer very good at keeping a poker face—because he was quick to add, "Of course, I don't expect you to make any decisions right this moment. The two of you need to think about this and talk it over, and ultimately, Tom, whatever you decide to do is fine. It's completely your decision."

Decision indeed. The only decision is whether it's better to suffer longer...or not so long. "Thank you, doctor."

Chapter Ten

Into the Darkness

What he found gave him the most difficulty was not the thought of the cancer spreading within him like a wildfire but the awareness—grown more acute than it had ever been in his life—that the past was irretrievable, and that each moment he had looked forward to and lived as fully as he could was present only for that moment before it moved beyond him into the past, where it could be recalled but not relived, remembered—perhaps with tears of joy and loss—but not regained. *It could not be held onto.* And those moments that he had most regretted had also moved beyond him and could not be reshaped or undone. What gave him the most difficulty was this heightened understanding of time itself, its brevity and its endlessness, its presence and its absence, its unrelenting advance and its inescapable retreat, and his own inability to control anything about it.

He remembered one day when he went whitewater canoeing with a friend and the canoe capsized, the two of them slipping into the darkness of the river in such a languorous manner it seemed nothing dangerous was happening, when abruptly he found himself swept underwater by the powerful current and slammed up against a submerged tree trunk, unable to move, the surface clear and tantalizing a foot or so above him, beyond that the sky a kind of lucent milky white, while below where the force of the river was pulling him down and where he knew there was a network of branches, all was dark and obscure. He had plenty of time to think while he was pressed against the trunk, and it came to him as a startling revelation that this was it, he was going to die right here in the river because he could expect no mercy from that which possessed neither consciousness nor compassion, and therefore not even the conscience of a bully, only the indifferent and impartial application of force, and he was startled too at how quickly he went from believing himself in control of his life to believing himself completely and utterly without control. After the initial panic passed he was filled with the most profound sense of loss and sadness he had ever felt because he *knew* he was about to die, sadness for all that he would never experience, for the marriage to Fran that he would never see grow and mature (they were newlyweds at the time), for the fatherhood he would never have and the children he would never see, for all that he might contribute to the world and to other people in his life, for the simple fact that he would not be able to accomplish any of what he wanted to accomplish in life because here it was, over, finished, ended long before he had ever expected it would end, and he could do nothing about it. And then he was out of the river somehow, he had found a purchase and pulled himself out, or something had given way and released him, he did not really know, he knew only that he was free and he was above water breathing, and there too was his friend, gray-faced and looking half dead, absent the glasses he had started out with, hair plastered down on his forehead and cheeks, but above water and alive, as he himself was.

What he drew from the river on that day—besides the unexpected gift of his life—was a resolution that he must not take anything for granted, that each moment was precious and not to be wasted, and that beneath all the cliches about time flying and life being too short and the need to seize the day was the simple truth that when he was trapped underwater, in those throbbing lucid moments of apprehension, *he had thoroughly believed he was about to die,* long, long before he had ever expected to, and no amount of rationalization afterwards would ever convince him the truth was otherwise. And thus he had an obligation to himself above all to live every moment of his life fully, as much as he could possibly manage, as much as was possible, to live every moment consciously, to be in the present and not wish he were elsewhere doing something other than what he was doing, to *choose* being in the moment and to make the moment have meaning, to *create joy* wherever and whenever he could, in the beating of his heart, in the drawing of each breath, in the consciousness of being alive, because to wish for something else when he had the power to control the moment and when he now *knew*—not just intellectually but in his heart—that that power could be wrenched from him in an instant was to waste his life.

But still, somehow, despite what he thought were his best efforts, he found himself having to relearn the same lessons again and again and again as the years went by, as though like a dimwitted child he were incapable of understanding them for more than a few moments. Still, somehow, the present had largely eluded him, he had not lived up to the expectations he had set for himself, he had frittered away years of his life as though he had an unlimited supply of them, and now he was faced again with the dark force and he knew—as surely as he had known when he was in the river—he would not escape it. *This* time he would not escape it.

He was tormented equally by memories of joy and by memories of sorrow and regret because in either case he was forced to recognize the undeniable fact that they represented the *past,* and the past was gone, as completely as when July fireworks lit up the night sky for a few moments and then disappeared, absorbed back into that darkness which was both the foil for their brilliance and the source of their issue. Whether he remembered the rapture of his wedding day, when he and Fran consumed a bottle of champagne on the short car ride from the wedding to the reception and her smile could not possibly have been any wider or brighter; or the missed opportunity of being "King for the Day" in Ben's second grade class (where, according to a disappointed Ben, the moms and dads who came in as invited readers were provided with a crown and a velvet cape and a throne upon which to sit and read to the class), he felt equally the sense of time gone by, of moments lost, painful phantom feelings for the past like those described by amputees for their missing limbs. But the difference between now and then was that in those days there were always new things to *look forward to*. Even after the lessons he learned through his brush with death in the river (those lessons he had to learn *repeatedly),* if a moment of great joy faded into the past or he missed an opportunity to do something unique, he took solace in the belief that there would be other chances. The future offered limitless new prospects and abundant time for healing and atonement. Now there would be no more chances, and whatever he had not done, whatever failures he had been guilty of or opportunities he had missed, whatever joys he had neglected to recognize or to seize were lost for all time. He had nothing to look forward to now except his own death, and he found himself terrified at the prospect of feeling joy because he knew it would be gone in an instant, gone forever.

Despite the cynicism that came so naturally to him, for much of his life he had sustained himself with things to look forward to, fishing and skiing trips, summer vacations, traveling with Fran, new architectural projects, dinners with friends, spending time with grandchildren—events large or small, it didn't matter which, so long as they served the purpose of moving him forward—but only now was he beginning to understand why: *the present became the past too quickly.* Unless you looked at something up ahead it was impossible to hold onto what you saw. It was like driving in a speeding car and trying to focus your vision on an object adjacent to you. You couldn't do it. You were forced either to look ahead or behind if you hoped to see the object for more than an instant, as something more than a blur. So acute was his sense of time passing that he began to dread moments of joy, because even before they happened he anticipated their movement into the past and mourned their loss, and in the very moments when he felt joy most deeply he was already noting its passage, thinking *it's gone already,* and feeling a kind of sorrow at least as painful as whatever pleasure he felt.

And so for a long while, weeks perhaps (he did not know, he had lost all track of time), he found himself living in a kind of limbo, outside of time, in a place where the past was too painful to recall and the present became the past too quickly and the future held nothing for him to look forward to. He became a prisoner without a cell, without walls or boundaries, without moorings or direction, and his truest companion was the sadness that accompanied him every moment of every day. His bamboo fly rod, which he had started refinishing to give to Ben, sat in the corner of the workroom out of its rod case, broken down into sections which lay unfinished and neglected. He no longer had any desire to complete it. Like every building he had ever designed and built it would merely fall apart over time and disintegrate into dust. He no longer had any desire to see his son or his grandson either—it was too painful, they represented all that would be lost—which only intensified the sadness in his heart. There was too much pain in the world, too much loss. There was *only* loss, really. *To be alive meant to lose everything, sooner or later.* Life was a kind of constant shedding or casting off, an indiscriminate passing away of all that had meaning along with all that had none, a daily forced lesson in accepting loss, in learning to let go of what could not be held onto, a reproof against the belief—the vain and childish belief—that joy could last for anything more than a moment. And when you understood that you understood that it was gone even *in* the moment, and if it was gone *in* the moment, *it never really existed.* Doctors had become very proficient at easing physical pain, they had pushed his own pain far enough to the periphery of consciousness that it no longer concerned him, but neither they nor anyone else could lessen the pain pressing in around his heart. Neither they nor anyone else could usher him out of the dark place in which he found himself, where there was nothing to do but wait for the end.

"Ben, I'm very worried about your father. I think he's given up." Fran had not wanted to lay this burden on her son. He had enough to worry about with still being in his first year of teaching and having a second child on the way. But she had reached the point where she could no longer face Tom's sadness alone. It hurt too much for her to see him this way, and, more importantly, she felt incapable now of bringing him up out of it by herself. If he were to have any hope of finding comfort or pleasure in what remained of his life (*years!* she still hoped and prayed for), she must admit she could not do it alone.

"What makes you say that, Mom?"

With the unrelenting urgencies of preparing for classes, reading stacks of papers, and Marie's pregnancy, he had not been over to see his father in quite some time. Marie was only a little more than six months along and still working full time for the educational testing company she had started with two years ago, but she was already quite large, and seemed to need a good deal more rest than she did when she was pregnant with Teddy, which meant that he was assuming more of the child care and food prep duties of late. Added to his routines of working out and playing a little tennis, and to his and Marie's getting together with friends occasionally, he had little extra time, and he felt guilty that he hadn't spent any of it thinking about his father lately.

"He didn't want me to tell you this because, well, you know how he is. He doesn't want to be the center of attention. He doesn't want to have to put anyone out at all, but the pain started coming back again and his PSA level has gone way up. The doctor says he needs to be getting radiation to control the pain, and maybe even chemotherapy, but he wants no part of it. He's been feeling nauseated to the point where he hardly eats anything anymore. He rarely gets out of bed at all, just stays in the bedroom watching TV, says it's the only thing he can do now. But he's not really watching it. And he's not reading, either...Ben, I think he's just waiting to die."

He could hear the fear in his mother's voice growing so soft and tremulous as she spoke these last few words that his heart ached for her. Then as he listened to her muffled sobbing he realized that as much as he had not paid enough attention to his father in recent weeks, he had also neglected his mother. The battle was not his father's alone, she too was suffering, perhaps as profoundly as his father was, and yet he was only now beginning to understand this fully.

"Mom, I'm sorry."

"It's not your fault, Ben. It's not *anybody's* fault. It's just...it's just I feel so helpless. I want to take his pain away, and I can't. And it's not just physical pain, it's more than that, I *know* it is. Something's bothering him that he won't let go of and he won't talk about."

"But I haven't been around much lately. I should have been more involved...for *both* of you."

"Ben, please, blaming yourself won't help. I'm not telling you any of this because I want you to feel bad. I just needed to let you know, I guess, more for myself than for anything else. I can't stand to see him in such pain, and I'm not ready for him to give up." She had been thinking of that more and more lately—the possibility of Tom's giving up completely—and what it would mean if he did. What would the future be like without him? She could get as far as asking the question, but she could not get beyond it. Beyond the question was a void, a blankness, that she was not yet ready to confront. They had known each other now for forty years, through *all* of her adulthood, really. Through marriage and child-rearing and now grandparenting, through all of the greatest joys of her life as well as the most profound challenges and transitions. How *could* she imagine what would lie ahead without him, in such *absence?*

"Would it help if I tried speaking to him?"

"It might. I don't know any more. I don't think it would hurt."

"Then I'll be right over."

"Ben?"

"What is it, Mom?"

"Please be gentle with him."

"I will, Mom. I will." The fact that she would even ask this of him suggested they had all moved into some new and unfamiliar territory, and he began to believe, to *feel,* for the first time—with sorrow and dread filling his heart—that his father was dying.

"He's in the bedroom," his mother said softly after they had greeted each other with a hug and he had followed her into the kitchen. "I haven't said anything to him about your coming over."

"Are you coming in too?"

"No. I'll wait out here."

The bedroom door was partly closed and the TV was turned on but otherwise the room was dark. Images from a show he recognized as WHO'S LINE IS IT, ANYWAY? flickered on the screen, but apparently the volume had been muted because there was no sound, and the resulting form of mime made the actors appear even more absurd than they were typically. He knocked lightly and opened the door a little wider. "Dad?"

"Who's that?"

"It's me, Dad," he said as he poked his head into the room. "Were you asleep? Am I waking you?"

"Oh, Ben, it's you," his father said in a voice that was barely audible. "Come in."

The bedcovers were rumpled and only partly covered his father's torso. He reached for his father's right hand and held it for a moment in both of his own, disturbed by the physical changes he was seeing. His father's face was pale and gaunt, and although he had clearly lost a significant amount of weight there was a flaccid, soft quality to his flesh, especially around his chest and mid-section, which was bloated well beyond its normal size. Ben thought of how much pride his father had always taken in keeping himself fit, and to see how far his father had fallen from the trim, confident man he had *always* been shook him deeply. He had come over to see his father—despite his mother's admonition—with a certain amount of anger built up inside him. The thought that his father might be closing himself off to life, with Teddy already a part of that life and another grandchild on the way, rekindled some of the same feelings of resentment that had smoldered in him for years. But to see him the way he was now—so weak and beaten down, so *pathetic* really (he would never have believed it possible that this word could describe his father; *distant, remote, detached,* absolutely; *arrogant* and *cold-hearted,* all too often true; but never *pathetic;*

his father was being not just humbled but *humiliated* by this disease)—drained all the anger away and transformed it in a way that he could not quite define, but he knew it had something to do with fairness. What was happening to his father was *wrong*. What was happening should not happen to anyone, but especially not to his father.

"How are you feeling, Dad?"

A wan smile spread from his father's lips. "I've been better." Just speaking seemed to require a considerable effort from him. "How's Marie, and that young rascal of a grandson?"

"They're both doing well, although Marie has had some weight gain and some swelling in her hands and feet, which has her doctor a little concerned about a condition called 'pregnancy induced hypertension,' which can lead to preeclampsia. They're keeping a close eye on the situation because if it really turns into preeclampsia and becomes more severe, they may have to take the baby early. But for now she's just trying to get plenty of rest and be careful about her diet—she can't have too much salt, which of course she loves, because as *you* know all too well from your own experience, salt retains fluid. But otherwise she's feeling fine. She's pretty upbeat about the pregnancy."

His father seemed to be listening and following, though every once in a while his eyes would close and his brow would furrow as if from pain. "Marie's concerned about you, though, as we all are. Dad, Mom told me what's been happening with you lately. She says you've had pain again and should be getting radiation treatments."

He watched as his father closed his eyes, took a deep breath, and gave a long, weary sigh. But there was no other reply.

"Is it true you've been having pain again?"

His father nodded but did not open his eyes.

"Are you in pain right now?"

Another nod, this time almost imperceptible.

"Then why won't you take the steps that will help you?"

This time the eyes opened and his father looked at him with an expression that seemed beyond tired, seemed exhausted, forlorn. "What's the point, Ben? What's the point?"

They gazed at each other for a protracted moment, each trying to understand the other, before the eyelids drifted shut once more, and Ben could feel welling up inside him all the accumulated anger of the years and the injustice of his father's pain and the certain future of a lifetime of absence and loss, and it all became too great for him to bear.

"Because people love you and don't want to see you in pain. Because your suffering isn't necessary. Because it isn't fair to Mom to quit now, not this way. Because it might help you to live longer, long enough and well enough to see your second grandchild born. Because...because Dad, I don't want to see you die!"

When he said this he could feel his chest swelling and his eyes filling with tears, a sob rising up from somewhere deep inside him, and he felt at once a kind of embarrassment for losing control in such a manner—he could not remember the last time he had cried—and yet also a kind of peacefulness, a sense of relief, washing through him that left him feeling clean and spent. "Can't you understand any of that?"

His father's eyes were open again and gazing sorrowfully at him. Then his father's hand was reaching forward and Ben bent toward it and curled into the side of his father's body, where the caress of his father's hand on his head made him feel like a child again.

Ben's words brought back the enormous regret that had been gnawing away at him for so many years now—that he had not been able to make Ben understand what was really inside him. The problem, he knew, was not Ben's but his own. Words had always failed him, had always come out twisted into some form of criticism of Ben that betrayed the truest feelings of his heart. And so for a time his despondence grew even greater, haunted him whether he was awake or asleep, in his dreams and in all of his most lucid moments, until at last he wanted to cry out to whomever or whatever, *why this pain? why nothing but this pain?* And it occurred to him suddenly that if joy could not exist for more than a moment, if, as he had surmised, it was gone even in the moment, and if this realization had been the source of his pain and had combined with all of his regret to deepen and intensify the pain, how was it that the pain endured? *How could joy be nothing but an illusion but pain an unending reality?* There was no answer to this, and the injustice of it tormented him until another thought finally surfaced into consciousness: *I created the pain,* followed close after by the inevitable conclusion: *I am the only one who can end it.* The more fully he understood this the more firmly he resolved that if he was going to die, he was not going to die this way, with such terrible regret. He was going to do something about it. When Ben was a young teen he used to preach to him a line from Julius Caesar that he had maintained as one of the few articles of his generally faithless life ever since he had first read it in college: "The fault, dear Brutus, is not in our stars but in ourselves that we are underlings." Now he was going to follow what he preached. He was going to do something about his regret even if it was too late to make any difference. He was going to look forward to the birth of his new grandchild and live to see him or her born even if joy was nothing but an illusion. He was not going to give in, finally, to the cynicism of pain without recognizing that it was as much an illusion as anything else he might believe he was feeling.

Chapter Eleven

Searching for Joy

Tom began the radiation treatments fully aware that the prospect of a cure—barring a miracle—was almost nonexistent. He now knew and accepted the fact that the radiation treatments, in the parlance of the medical world, were "palliative" and not "curative," and for that reason decided not to undergo chemotherapy also. He did not want to have to endure the side effects of chemo with only the most remote conceivable possibility that it could stop the cancer. He knew that he had entered territory the doctors were unfamiliar with— he could read between the lines of their words, Dr. Marshall's and the others', well enough to know they had no idea whether chemo would have any positive effects at all, but the negative effects were all too easily predictable, and he no longer wanted anything to do with negative effects. There had been enough of those already in his life, and his new resolve was to seek whatever was positive in life, to make whatever time he had left as full and complete as possible. By the same reasoning he had no desire to waste time castigating himself over whether or not he had been a fool for waiting so long to see a doctor about the problems he had kept hidden. Maybe if he had seen a doctor sooner and the cancer had been detected earlier, his fate would be different today—in all likelihood, that was the truth. But he could not worry about that any more. His days were limited, and there was no point in spending those days wallowing in regret (they had *always* been limited, but except for his brief epiphany underwater, he had never quite appreciated this fact fully, and so he could not waste time berating himself for this either because he had never been faced with it in such clear and starkly certain terms). Instead, he would begin to try to celebrate. Though he was not sure where or how he would start or where it would lead him, he would search for those things in his life that gave him the deepest and most profound pleasure—past, present, or future, it didn't matter—and try with every bit of strength he had left to stay focused on them, to hold them in his heart in a way that somehow fixed them there, kept them safe from the erosive influence of time, so that all that was good and meaningful would fill him and all that was petty and insignificant would be driven further and further away, to the margins of his being and beyond, as pure water poured long enough into a cup of sludge will eventually fill the cup with nothing but pure water.

And so each day, despite all the medications and the needle sticks and the radiation treatments and whatever else others deemed critical to continuing his life and his physical well being, his freedom from pain, he sought ways to celebrate. It was as though there were two battles being waged—the one on the outside conducted by others to insure that his body lived on, and the one on the inside that he was conducting by himself, alone and away from the view of everyone else, including even his dearest Fran, to find all that he cherished, all that gave his life meaning, all that was worth salvaging of his sixty years on earth, to find, utimately, the value of his existence, and then, as much as was humanly possible, to hold onto it and revel in it.

He began to do this in two ways. First, he resumed the work of restoring his bamboo fly rod for Ben. Each day he would hobble out to his workshop in the garage and, for as long as he could physically endure it, he would toil away at the task of transforming his old, worn cane rod into something he could feel satisfied enough with to hand over to Ben. With slow and painstaking precision he used a razor to strip the guide foot wraps and the guides themselves, scraped away old varnish from the ferrule wraps, then used a fine steel wool to polish the male ferrules and beeswax to snug up their fit into the female ferrules. Then he took thread and tape and a bobbin to wrap new guides carefully into place and applied new coats of varnish to bring out the luster of the bamboo, using dip tubes instead of a brush to make sure the finish appeared smooth and professional. He spent many hours over the course of a couple weeks using extra fine sandpaper to sand the cork handle, which had become dark and grimy over the years, into the pale blond color of a handle that looked new. As he labored he felt a kind of reverence for what he did, held the sections of the rod in his hands as though they were pieces of something sacred that warranted his utmost respect and vigilance and required all the care and deference he could bring to his work—not only to ensure the safe reconstruction and passage of the rod to Ben so that he could use it to fish, but because something elemental in the rod itself, in the sleek clean golden beauty of the bamboo, seemed to him alive, or imbued in some way with the essence of life, and thus obliged him with all the gravity, all the significance, all the responsibility of nourishing and restoring life to a living thing.

Even as he worked so assiduously each day on the fly rod, for the first time in his life he also began to keep a journal. As an architect he had routinely kept diligent notes and records about the thinking and planning involved in his work, but even though there was imagination and creativity in such writing, it was all professional in nature, steeped in the realms of geometry, logic and order. He had never broached the personal side of his life at all, had never—or so he thought then—had time for such a luxury when there were more pragmatic things to be thinking and writing about. Now that he had the time—or had very little time, depending upon how he chose to view it—he wondered how he could have done without keeping a journal for so much of his life. Now such writing helped him to focus and reflect upon all that seemed to him most important. The journal became indispensible to him as a source of honesty and insight. One day he would write about something from the distant past like the time when he was a child of four or five and had thrown a large rock at a frog. The rock had crushed the frog and killed it instantly, but the sight of its death was gruesome: the frog's intestines and stomach had been disgorged through its mouth, leaving him to wonder in despair why he had done this to such an innocent and unsuspecting creature. The frog had done nothing to him at all, nothing to threaten or hurt him, and he had killed it in a horrible way. Why? There was no reason, none, and he was so troubled by it that he confessed it tearfully later that night to his mother, and tucked it away in his heart along with the pledge to himself that he would never do anything like that again. In writing about it he realized that he had probably thrown the rock at the frog simply out of the morbid curiosity to see what would happen, not sure of the consequences, but beyond the grotesque physical consequence to the frog—which he had not bargained for and was not prepared for—was the profound confrontation with death itself, perhaps his first real confrontation with it, and more than that, with meaningless cruelty, which was all the worse because he had discovered such cruelty within himself.

Another day he would write about something from the more recent past like the trip he and Fran had taken to Montreal a few years ago in mid-June for a conference he was attending there. So many images and sensations flooded his mind as he wrote that he had trouble keeping pace: the setting sun glistening pink and lavender on the glass of one of Montreal's lovely modern buildings, sharply defined against a backdrop of brilliant blue sky; lush green parks and colorful flowers in the midst of towering glass skyscrapers and ancient stone edifices whose endurance he found inspiring; efficient and aesthetic use of underground mall space for retail shops in the heart of the city; couples too numerous to count strolling hand-in-hand (as they themselves were doing) and laughing to each other amid the throngs of people striding briskly or meandering leisurely along the sidewalks of Rue Ste. Catherine and Rue Peel on a balmy night, listening to the melodic riffs of streetcorner musicians playing jazz on their saxophones and trumpets; dining at intimate restaurants and outdoor cafes which they discovered serendipitously, one night happening upon a small place whose specialty was mussels, which they each tried prepared in different sauces and ate with their fingers, feeding each other samples and sopping up the delicious juices with fresh bread and washing it all down with bottles of wine; skipping conference sessions so that he and Fran could make love to each other more times in the space of a few days than they had done since they were in college. They had fallen in love once again while they were in Montreal (how many times in a lifetime could one fall in love with the same person? he wondered as he wrote), and had returned home feeling blessed and invigorated.

He wrote an entry about the time thirty years ago (which he remembered and felt in his heart as vividly as if it had been only last year) when he designed their house, their "home," and he and Fran did much of the work of building it, and about the excitement and passion they both felt daily as they looked back on the tangible progress of laying floors and raising up walls together. "Now remember, Tom," Fran used to say to him, "we're not just building any old house here, we're building a home, *our* home!" From the moment he began the process of thinking about what their home would look like, he knew it must be different from anything he had ever designed before. It must be functional, of course, but it must also have light, light throughout the house, and it must use that light for energy wherever possible. It must be built on the principles of function, aesthetics and energy conservation—they must harness the sun for light *and* warmth—and it must also fit within the landscape. The two-acre piece of property they had settled on was lovely in its own right, with a view of the river and a fine variety of trees, both deciduous and evergreen, some perhaps a century old, and he must fit the house within them without compromising their age and grace and without sacrificing the need for space and light, both inside *and* outside—and there must be space and light for a garden. *A garden was essential.* He loved the thought of growing things, and throughout the entire process of designing and building the house and fitting it within the landscape (what joy to work on such an architectural puzzle with your own land, your own future!) he imagined children— at least three of them, more if he could convince Fran of it— growing up within the house and a magnificent garden of vegetables and flowers flourishing outside of it. Looking back on it as he wrote, he realized that although some of it had not come true—they had only been able to have one child together—it was a time of his life he would not trade for anything, a time of such dreams and imagination, such anticipation of what the future held in store for them, such passion for life and work and love, that he would gladly live it all over again, *every moment of it.*

One day his writing led him to think about all the little things in life that were a source of joy to him, and he decided that he would try to catalog as many of them as he could, in part because the very act of doing so would give him pleasure; in part because he wanted to remember everything and forget nothing;

and in part because he hoped that identifying the smaller moments of joy would lead him to two greater rewards: first he would be able to *hold* all of these moments more fully, more consciously within himself at all times (he speculated, as he wrote, underlining the thought for emphasis, <u>CAN there be joy without consciousness of it?—or is joy, instead, an utter and absolute release, or absence, of consciousness?</u>); and second he would be able to understand some essential truth about joy that would help him to create it and experience it in every moment that he had left in his life.

As a way of constructing some sort of logic or order to what he wrote, he decided to arrange the content of his catalog by seasons, and wrote first about the spring:

- *o-ka-leeee* sound of red-winged blackbird as first harbinger of spring
- starting seed trays in Feb-March, and watching first sprouts come up, and transplanting them into the garden in April-May
- sweet taste of new maple syrup on pancakes
- peepers trilling in almost deafening chorus in early April
- pink lady-slippers in May-June
- Aaron Copland's *APPALACHIAN SPRING*, especially the first three minutes or so, which produce a feeling as close to holiness as anything I know
- leaves of the maple trees outside my study window dappled lemon-lime in the slant of spring sunlight, fluttering on the breeze like a thousand butterflies
- varied shades of green in lush woods.

For summer he wrote:

- dance of insects on an early summer evening in the light of the setting sun, swarming in a golden cloud of frenzied life
- large white mayflies ascending from the Connecticut River in Pittsburgh in June, at dusk, like thick white snowflakes not falling onto but arising up from the river, and trout snapping the surface of the water and leaping clear out of it to snatch them away
- fireflies magically lighting up the dark out on the porch on warm summer nights, with Ben sitting in my lap
- rustle of leaves (poplar) in the early morning breeze of a July day
- deep bass primal calls of bullfrogs, more urgent and insistent, more unrelenting, as the summer night deepens
- electric sizzle of cicadas on a steamy summer day
- tomatoes from the garden, sliced red and juicy and sprinkled with a bit of salt and pepper and fresh basil (one of the most marvelous smells on earth!), and native corn slathered in butter
- cigar and Benedictine on the screen porch on summer evenings, watching the sun sink below the horizon and the brilliant pinks and oranges fade to lavender and purple and finally gray, listening all the while to the bullfrogs and the sounds of night falling.

For the fall he wrote:

- cool, crisp autumn air and the need for flannel shirts, sweaters, jackets

- touch and feel of flesh becoming cool and dry, silky, after the mugginess of summer
- first smell of smoke from a wood-burning stove
- clarity of blue sky—deeper and sharper cerulean blue than any other time of year
- colors, colors colors!—swamp maple reds and birch yellows and countless hues of orange and salmon and the burgundy shades of oak that come later, all against the backdrop of green grass, fields of goldenrod and azure blue skies
- quality of quiet in the early morning when I go out to get the newspaper, a kind of wistful quiet, or absence of sound, once the raucous spring/summer serenades and complaints of courting and competing birds have departed
- burning leaves in the fall, mounds of them piled high and flaming, the rich smoke laden with memories of Halloween and cool crisp air
- pumpkins! and pumpkin pie, and the continued harvesting of vegetables from the garden as green peppers ripen on the vine into sweet red peppers

He never got to winter, per se, because his strategy soon began to fail. One category would lead to another (Copland's *APPALACHIAN SPRING*, which he listened to almost exclusively in the spring, led him to want to write about *music*, which was its own category and had no season); or an item might not have a specific season (the smell of a newly opened can of coffee); or the mere mention of Ben or Fran in a sentence would launch him into thinking about them; or an item might describe a specific place at a specific moment in time (moon over the ocean in Bermuda), while another might be true for every year (*o-ka-leeee* of red-winged black); and so the very nature of restricting himself to such an order seemed contrary to what he was trying to do, which was to capture the essence of what gave him joy, and that essence, it now seemed, was at one and the same time fleeting and ephemeral and random, reliant upon serendipity, and also predictable and dependable and enduring, reliant upon the earth revolving with mechanical certainty each day in a precise path around the sun. So he decided to abandon categories altogether and simply add to his list in whatever fashion thoughts came to him and celebrate each item for itself independent of any category or structure. He wrote the heading "Miscellaneous Joys" atop the page of the journal that began his running list and included entries like

- feel of freshly laundered clothing, especially denim pants and broadcloth cotton shirts
- smell of coffee when the can is first opened, nose just above the dark grounds, inhaling deeply
- touch and feel of Ben's, and later Teddy's, tiny soft infant fingers coiled around my index finger
- listening to Debussy's *LA MER* in the summertime, the swirling rhythms of the music like the shifting currents of the ocean
- listening *anytime* to the Ode to Joy movement in Beethoven's *NINTH SYMPHONY*
- cool snap in August at the ocean—air brisk and clear, blue sky sharply delineating leaves, blades of grass, rose hips—a harbinger of fall that might last a day or two, perhaps a week, but surely a preview of the halcyon days ahead
- smell of freshly mown grass
- melodic song of the wood thrush, like flute music coming from the deep woods at dawn and in the early evenings of summer

- full moon rising white and clear and enormous above the Atlantic Ocean when we were at the beach after Ben was born, Fran and Ben curled into sleep together inside the cottage while I sat outside watching the moon rise, its reflection shimmering and dancing in a thousand particles of light upon the sea, like diamonds, and the promise of the future, of Ben's life, immense, limitless, unbounded.

He felt an almost triumphant kind of freedom each time he added an item to the list, as though by thinking of it and writing it down he were adding to a growing store of happiness that could not be lost or taken away, liberating and celebrating what was truest and best about himself, his life, his awareness of the world outside that would continue to exist beyond him forever as well as the world inside, to the depths of his soul, the core of his being, which would depart when he departed but that might at least be glimpsed by the words he wrote, so that his son and perhaps his grandson too would know a little of who he was at his very best, would know that underneath whatever else they might think of him there was a man who sought to love life.

One day when he added to his list...

- smell of salty sea air before even seeing the source
- first sight of the vast blue panorama that is the ocean
- ceaseless furl and crash of the waves, rhythmic and reassuring

...he realized that his list could be endless, that it *was* endless, and if that were true then how he viewed each moment of life became a matter of choice, of *choosing what to make each moment mean.*

For a while this thought gave him great comfort, helped him to believe that despite his inability to control the cancer ravaging his body, he could at least control the time he had remaining, he could make the time meaningful and positive; but even in the midst of it he could feel another thought nagging at him, pulling him away from his comfort and supplanting it with something dark and haunting that he had been steadfastly avoiding. If his joys could be viewed as limitless couldn't the same be said of the petty dissatisfactions and complaints and abuses he had been guilty of during the course of his life? Hadn't he, after all, *chosen*—far too often—the *opposite* of joy, whatever it might be called...unhappiness? dissatisfaction? misery? sorrow? *Hadn't he chosen to be brutal to Ben and unfaithful to Fran?*

There it was, out in the open, the thought that had been lurking on the periphery just beyond sight of everything he had written, but he could not write it down in his journal, it was too painful, too shameful, too difficult to put into the concrete form of words on a page that he must look at and that others might discover. To put it into such a stark, unvarnished admission of truth was not a choice he could make, but to leave it out and continue writing as though it did not exist was also, now, no longer a choice he could make. And so he ceased writing in his journal altogether, but the thoughts and memories engendered by his realization came at him again and again, tormenting him, and he found that what had started out as a means of celebration had been transformed into a kind of self-loathing that he could neither express nor choose to avoid.

Memories came to him now unbidden. He remembered the affairs he had had with women he thought he had forgotten about, back in his twenties and thirties when he was still acting out the myth of "TD, the Score King," back when he was still too ignorant to appreciate fully what he had in Fran, and each time he remembered he felt again the anguish of failing to live up to the standards of self-control and honesty he believed in, and the shameful sense of betrayal at the thought of how much Fran had given of herself to him in all their years together and how much he truly loved her. He remembered things he had said to Ben that no father should ever say to his son, like the time when Ben was probably only seven or eight and he had called Ben a "stupid son-of-a-bitch" for leaving some tools out in the rain, and accused him of being "lazy and completely without ambition" another time when Ben, as a teenager, was slow to find a summer job. Once, after Ben had rear-ended another car and caused over two thousand dollars worth of damage to his prized Porsche, instead of being the patient, understanding father he aspired to be at such a time, he had looked at Ben with disgust and said, "You'd fuck up a wet dream."

The more he remembered of his failures and his shortcomings the more he realized how much deception had been a fundamental part of his life. Threaded throughout his adult life had been a pattern of deception that undercut everything he thought was good and decent in him. All along he had deluded himself with the thought that he was in control of what he was doing, when all along the opposite had been true. He had been deceiving those he cared most about in life, and worst of all, he had been deceiving himself. *His life had been a lie.*

When Ben received the call from his mother that his father had taken a terrible turn for the worse he was deeply shaken, all the more so because the doctors had decided just yesterday that it was too dangerous to wait any longer to take the baby given

Marie's worsening condition: they must take the baby right away. *Today.*

For several weeks his father had had a wonderful rebound and it had almost seemed the cancer was in remission. His father's energy level was greater than it had been for months, his overall state of mind more upbeat than Ben had ever seen it. Each time Ben saw him he was amazed by the transformation: the sharp, often bitter and ironic edge of his father's humor had disappeared altogether, replaced by a softer side that Ben had only rarely glimpsed—and then, for the most part, only as it was directed to Marie and Teddy. His mother reported that his father was working each day on a "secret" project out in his workshop, and that he was actually keeping a journal, writing in it daily, and taking great pleasure in doing so. She said he grew tired each day, of course, but based on what Ben saw for himself as well as the reports she gave him, it seemed that something almost miraculous was happening to his father.

Then without warning it had changed. For no apparent reason his father had stopped writing and had begun spending more and more time sitting in his study just looking out the window, or in bed sleeping again as he had done before the turnaround. It was different this time in that his father showed no evidence of physical pain, nor did he report any, and his general attitude and demeanor displayed a kind of tolerance, or acceptance, that had been missing before. The anger and bitterness were gone—Ben had seen this for himself—but for the past few weeks now he had known that his father was slipping again. He was eating little or nothing at all and having difficulty speaking, his proud frame withering away more, it seemed, every day. Hospice had started coming to the house, and Ben had begun stopping in daily to visit with his father or, if his father was too tired for a visit, to speak with his mother.

Still, when her call came it was a shock to him. Just the day before he had told both parents of the plan to induce labor in Marie today, and although his father had not said anything, had merely nodded and smiled before closing his eyes, the thought had never occurred to Ben that his father might not live to see his new grandchild born.

"I'm so sorry to be calling you, Ben," his mother had said, and he could hear the sorrow and desperation in her unsteady voice. "I know you're with Marie for what should be a joyful event, and I've been wrestling with whether or not to call, but I finally decided to do what I thought you would want me to do. I'm sorry, I'm so sorry."

"Mom, what is it? What's wrong?" he had said, knowing there could be only one reason for her to be calling him now.

"I don't know if your father will last through the day. His breathing is terrible. Oh, I'm so sorry to be calling you."

"Mom, it's okay. You did the right thing. I would have wanted you to call. Is there anyone there with you now."

"Yes, a nurse from hospice is here."

"Is he conscious at all?"

"No, he hasn't been for some time."

"Please talk to him for me. Tell him I'll be over as soon as I can. Maybe he'll hear you. Tell him I love him."

"I will. You take care of Marie and that new baby," she managed to get out before she broke down completely.

"I will, Mom. I will. I love you. I'll be there as soon as I can. Goodbye."

He felt as if he were drifting at sea in a dense fog and Ben's muffled voice was calling to him, "Dad, can you hear me?" and he could hear himself calling back, "I'm here, I'm right here," but his voice was being absorbed by the fog like something liquid being drawn into a sponge, so he stopped trying to speak and merely nodded.

"He's nodding. He's trying to say something, I know he is." Of course I am, Fran. There's so much I want to say, to both of you. So much. For one thing, you have been my lover, my best friend, my wife, my soul mate, the mother of my child, the most loyal person to me on earth, the one I love the most—you have been *everything* to me, and I don't think I've ever told you this, I don't think you know it. For another, *there must always, finally, be a reckoning. Always.* I thought I knew that, but now I know I didn't.

"I just came from the hospital, Dad. Marie just gave birth to our beautiful new baby boy, Michael Thomas Derringer, your new grandson."

He remembered Ben's birth again as he had so many times over the years, felt again the flood of anguish at Fran's pain and the overwhelming joy at seeing his son for the first time, and he wanted to tell Ben about this, the joy, and how he should try never to lose it in his life, never to forget it, or through cowardice or neglect or personal ambition turn it into something he might later regret, as he himself had done, because there must always be a reckoning, and the pain of that reckoning just might be more than he could bear.

Fran daubed at a tear forming in his eye. "Ben, I know he's hearing you. Keep talking to him. Please, please help him to get through."

"Marie is doing fine, Dad. And we can't wait for you to see him. He looks just like you."

My son! O, my son! I want to sing to you! he thought, Ben lying unfolded and motionless in the sun, stretched out in his crib in blissful sleep warm and pink and peaceful, *I want to sing of generation and regeneration, of my father and his father, my son and your son, of life and birth, spring and sighing trees, of your sister or sisters and brother or brothers to be, of continuity and hope, and joy so powerful it brings me to tears, of love and self-sacrifice, of fruition and fulfillment, change and changelessness, of the brevity of life and the endlessness of time and possibility. O, if only I could hold such thoughts within me forever I would sing such a song to you as has never been heard before!* But he had not done it. He had wanted to in that moment—all of his heart and his mind and his will were united in wanting to in that moment—but he had not done it. He had failed.

"Can you imagine the fishing trips we'll be able to take now, Dad? There'll be four of us. You'll have to teach him, of course, just as you've been teaching Teddy, but he'll learn. You're such a wonderful teacher."

He had wanted to, but he had failed. He had even tried—in his mind and in his heart he had tried—but it had come out all jumbled and confused, not at all what he had intended. And so he must live with that. Or die with that, for that was what was happening now. He was dying. And the realization came to him not with the terror it had once possessed but as a kind of curiosity because there was still time, there was still time to make amends.

"He wants to say something. Oh, Ben, he's trying so hard. Tom, it's all right to let go. Please, please let go. We'll be all right. Ben will be with me, and I'll have two lovely grandchildren to dote on and tell stories to."

"I'll tell them all about you, Dad. They'll always know what a wonderful grandfather they had. And don't worry about Mom. I'll take care of her."

I know you will, my boy. I know you will. But you're not the problem. You've never been the problem, and I have failed in that too. Please forgive me.

"Dad, somehow I've never been able to say I love you. I don't know why. I'm sorry. But you need to know that. I love you."

[192]

From a distance somewhere above he could see that Fran was caressing his face and Ben was holding his hand, drawing close to his lips, through which he was trying to speak.

"I think he's saying 'forget.'"

Forgive me. Please forgive me, for I am failing even now.

"We'll never forget, Dad. Never."

He could feel himself smiling, thinking *I tried, at least I tried,* even as Ben's grip on his hand tightened and his awareness of it began to fade. All was becoming light, what he saw and what he felt, as though the sensations of sight and touch had become one and the same, and all weight left him and he could feel himself floating, drifting toward something he recognized at first with a sense of welcome and relief, and his heart began swelling at the recognition with all the joy and sorrow he had ever felt in his life, with the powerful push of the life force toward light and sunshine and its inherent sense of sacred obligation to carry life forward, to think positively if one must think at all, to *move,* to sustain oneself and to prosper and to generate new life and to sustain and nurture and honor and celebrate that life also, and swelling too with the contradictory but equally powerful pull of death toward darkness and rest and cessation, and its inherent sense of inevitability and the need to acknowledge and accept and even welcome the sacred precept that all life must come to end, and to impart to those who remain behind that death too must be honored and celebrated, and he could feel himself reaching out to embrace all of what swelled his heart as he took one last breath and thought with joy *I am gone.*

About the Author

Tim Barretto teaches writing, speaking, and literature at the University of New Hampshire's Thompson School of Applied Science. He and colleague Kate Hanson co-founded the Community Leadership program at the school in 2001 as a way of helping students inter-

ested in becoming activists and community leaders to find and develop their voices. His creative work includes short stories published in literary journals and a one-act play about bullying that was performed at several schools in New Hampshire's Strafford County. He has spent most of his adult life pursuing ways to eliminate child abuse, and in that pursuit has served as a passionate advocate for children. When he has free time, he loves to spend it outdoors fishing, hiking, or skiing with family and friends. He lives in Dover, New Hampshire, with his wife, Mary.